HARLEQUIN

D0051542

Natalie Anderson

BOUGHT: ONE NIGHT, ONE MARRIAGE

HARLEQUIN® *Presents*

Glamorous international settings...
unforgettable men...passionate romances—
Harlequin® Presents® promises you the world!

HPATM1208

HARLEQUIN®
Presents

Welcome to the December 2008 collection of Harlequin Presents!

This month, be sure to read Lynne Graham's *The Greek Tycoon's Disobedient Bride,* the first book in her exciting new trilogy, VIRGIN BRIDES, ARROGANT HUSBANDS. Plus, don't miss the second installment of Sandra Marton's THE SHEIKH TYCOONS series, *The Sheikh's Rebellious Mistress.* Get whisked off into a world of glamour, luxury and passion in Abby Green's *The Mediterranean Billionaire's Blackmail Bargain,* in which innocent Alicia finds herself falling for hard-hearted Dante. Italian tycoon Luca O'Hagan will stop at nothing to make Alice his bride in Kim Lawrence's *The Italian's Secretary Bride,* and in Helen Brooks's *Ruthless Tycoon, Innocent Wife,* virgin Marianne Carr will do anything to save her home, and ruthless Rafe Steed is on hand to help her. Things begin to heat up at the office for interior designer Merrow in Trish Wylie's *His Mistress, His Terms,* when playboy Alex sets out to break all the rules. Independent Cally will have one night she'll never forget with bad-boy billionaire Blake in Natalie Anderson's *Bought: One Night, One Marriage.* And find out if Allie can thaw French doctor Remy de Brizat's heart in Sara Craven's *Bride of Desire.* Happy reading!

We'd love to hear what you think about Presents. E-mail us at Presents@hmb.co.uk or join in the discussions at www.iheartpresents.com and www.sensationalromance.blogspot.com, where you'll also find more information about books and authors!

Private jets. Luxury cars. Exclusive five-star hotels.
Designer outfits for every occasion and an
entourage of staff to see to your every whim....

In this brand-new collection, ordinary women
step into the world of the super-rich and are

He'll have her, but at what price?

This exciting new miniseries continues next
month with

Hotly Bedded, Conveniently Wedded
by Kate Hardy

Only from Harlequin Presents!

Natalie Anderson

BOUGHT: ONE NIGHT, ONE MARRIAGE

TAKEN BY THE
MILLIONAIRE

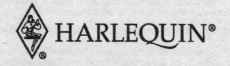
HARLEQUIN®

TORONTO • NEW YORK • LONDON
AMSTERDAM • PARIS • SYDNEY • HAMBURG
STOCKHOLM • ATHENS • TOKYO • MILAN • MADRID
PRAGUE • WARSAW • BUDAPEST • AUCKLAND

ISBN-13: 978-0-373-12785-6
ISBN-10:   0-373-12785-5

BOUGHT: ONE NIGHT, ONE MARRIAGE

First North American Publication 2008.

www.eHarlequin.com

Printed in U.S.A.

All about the author...
Natalie Anderson

Possibly the only librarian who got told off herself for talking too much, NATALIE ANDERSON decided writing books might be more fun than shelving them—and boy, was she right. Especially writing romance—it's the realization of a lifetime dream kick-started by many an afternoon spent devouring Grandma's Harlequin® novels.

She lives in New Zealand with her husband and four gorgeous but exhausting children. Swing by her Web site, at www.natalie-anderson.com, anytime—she'd love to hear from you.

I could try to write all the "whys" but there isn't enough room for all the words, so I'll keep it simple: For Mum—for everything.

CHAPTER ONE

'I CAN'T believe I agreed to come here.' Cally looked around her, slowly taking in the decadent atmosphere in the hip Sydney bar. It was like Bacchanalia—riotous revelry. There were well over one hundred women filling the place with laughter, leer and enough bling to blind the nation. Canapés were being consumed with glee and being washed down with terrifyingly neon concoctions. High-pitched chatter drowned the relentless deep thud, thud, thud of the music. Anticipation hung in the air. You could taste the excitement, the expectation of one hell of a good show.

Cally screwed up her nose.

'Oh, come on.' Mel looked at her with a 'get a grip' expression. 'It's for charity.'

'There are better ways of raising money for charity.'

'What's better than watching a line-up of the most eligible bachelors in town?'

'If they were that eligible they wouldn't be here.'

'What?'

'They must be the most conceited meat-heads to agree to participate.' The snark was enough to earn her another 'get over it' look.

'Don't be so uptight.' Mel shook her head disparagingly. 'You've been working way too hard. They're doing it to support a good cause. It's a laugh. *A laugh.*' Another pointed look. 'Remember how to do that? Open your mouth, go "ha ha"?'

'You know I'm damn good at laughing.' Cally sighed. 'I'm just not in the mood for this kind of funny tonight.'

'Well, down your Sex in the Surf or whatever that drink is called, and get yourself in the mood. Sit back, enjoy the show. Nobody says you have to bid. Buy a few raffle tickets and be done with it.'

Mel was right. But the scene didn't sit well with Cally. It was so far removed from the cause it was supposed to be supporting. Here they were, draped with all this money—conspicuous consumption to the max. Half these people probably wouldn't give a second thought to those who this event was supposed to be helping. They were paying lip service—just wanting to get together with a gang of girlfriends and ogle some talent. Bitch over someone else's dress. Out to outdo and be seen doing it.

It was the kind of thing her mother would love. She'd be here, out-glamorising even the most glamorous and providing sound bites in the style of a Miss Universe save-the-world speech. Fortunately she was away sunning herself on a beach in the Mediterranean somewhere.

Cally grimaced as she glanced round again. Nope. So not her scene. She preferred to stay out of the limelight her mother had always sought. Yes, she had money. Yes, she felt a responsibility to do charitable work. But her father had taught her how much more fun it was to *do* something behind the scenes, or to donate anonymously. When he died she'd made a vow to continue his work and so had maintained strong connections with his favourite charity—the homeless shelter only a few blocks from the opulent home in which she'd spent her happiest childhood years. She loved the time she put into it— feeling as if it was a way of retaining links with him, wanting to do something that she knew would have made him proud.

Mel cleared her throat and glared again. 'Must you be so earnest, Cally? For heaven's sake, have another drink. Or one of those chocolate truffles.'

Cally grinned at that. Actually the chocolate truffles were pretty divine. She pulled the plate nearer. Half the women here wouldn't touch them anyway, so Cally could have their share. Then she gave herself a rebuke over her pathetic holier-than-thou moment. Many of these women gave time as well as money to charity. One of the wealthiest women in the room spent a night a week answering calls on a youth helpline. And, while she might come across as if nothing mattered more than the colour of the dressing rooms in her new guest wing, the way she could listen to and calm distressed teens was incredible.

The music got even louder, and the MC appeared on stage. Applause filled the air. The show was about to start. Biting into another truffle, Cally sat back and acknowledged that maybe Mel was right. Man candy. So what if people were buying some hunky company? She wasn't shopping. She'd just watch, be amused by the craziness, try not to feel cheapened, buy a few raffle tickets and donate a chunk on the quiet later. She sipped from her wide-rimmed glass and as she relaxed the first man for sale appeared.

'I can't believe I agreed to come here.' Blake looked around him thunderstruck. 'I *know* I didn't agree to this.'

'You did.'

'I thought you meant some kind of working bee. You said a spot of gardening, cleaning up.'

'And that's exactly what you'll be doing.'

Blake gave Judith, his PA, a look of withering disbelief. Not if the sound of those braying women was anything to go by. 'I really don't think so.'

She'd insisted they come straight from the office, he'd been working late. So here he was after a long day, in his suit, needing a shave. He ran his fingers through his hair to stop him exiting the scene. For a second he wished he smoked so he could do something to relieve the stress. Honestly, meeting with a roomful of sceptical investors had nothing on this. This

sounded worse than a bear pit. Now he knew how those gla-
diators had felt back in the Roman days. The first poor guy had
gone on and the howls from the divas in the audience were
deafening. Then he heard the bidding begin and the feeling of
panic, mixed with distaste, rose.

'Give the organisers my apologies. I'll make a donation.
Large as you like. But I'm not sticking around for this.'

Judith blocked his exit from the room. Not hard given that
she was wider than a small van at the moment. She rubbed at
the swell of her belly and looked at him with the beseeching
eyes of a homeless puppy. Only hers were blue not brown and
there was an irrepressible twinkle in them. 'You're not really
going to leave, are you?'

He hesitated.

'You can't. I said you'd be here.' She switched to rubbing
the small of her back. The action pushed her belly out even
further. 'Blake, please. You promised.'

She wasn't laying it on with a trowel but by the wheelbar-
row. Dump truck even.

His eyes narrowed. 'The sooner you go on maternity leave,
the better.'

She smiled sweetly. 'I knew you wouldn't let me down.'

Like most men, Blake found it pretty difficult to say no to
the pleas of a pregnant woman. But while Judith knew she
could play on it, she didn't know the real reason why. There
wasn't much Blake wouldn't do to keep a pregnant woman
happy. He didn't want to bear any more of a burden than he
already did—one lost child was too much as it was.

He watched as she made her way to the door with her slower
than usual—but still pretty quick—gait. He hadn't been joking.
She might have been leaning on her pregnancy vulnerability
just then, but he'd noticed how tired she'd been these last
couple of weeks. Her husband was a fool. No wife of Blake's
would be working through her pregnancy—not any of it. She'd
be at home being cared for and not racing around.

He'd tried to lighten Judith's workload for her, but she'd laughed at him. Saying she was pregnant, not sick, and that she was as capable as ever of the multitude of tasks he required of her. And, employment law being what it was, he had to let her. He still thought her husband would have more ability to slow her down. But he was so besotted he said yes to anything. Whatever made her happy, made him happy. Blake grimaced. He couldn't ever see himself giving that kind of power to another. Self-sufficiency was the way to success.

Then again, hadn't he failed to say no to Judith just now? His frown deepened and his sympathy for her husband grew. Her maternity leave definitely couldn't come soon enough. And right now Blake had other things to worry about—like being paraded in front of a room full of women wanting to bid for the 'catch of the day'.

His turn edged closer. He went and stood in the wings, peeked through a tiny gap in the curtain out to the audience. He knew full well Judith had misled him about this 'charity fundraiser'. OK, not misled, but not filled in all the info on the page. He scanned the crowd. Women who'd probably never got their hands dirty. Never ever come into contact with the people this event was supposedly going to help. The homeless, the hopeless, the destitute, the desperate. They'd have no idea, here they were just doing their 'bit' for charity.

He listened to the high-pitched shrieks of laughter as the latest victim suffered the humiliation of being priced. This was shaping up to be one of the most embarrassing evenings of his life. But, as Judith had said, he'd made a promise and Blake McKay always kept his promises. He turned away from the audience, thrust back his shoulders and gave himself the pep talk. Whatever he did, he did to the best of his ability. This was how he'd climbed rung by rung from the bottom of the heap to the top. With sheer grit and determination to be the best. And so, if they wanted a man to perform, he'd be their man—their 'He-Slave'. He loosened his tie a little. Ran his fingers through his hair to give him even more of the tousled long-day-at-the-office look. He looked across the backstage area at a couple of the other poor souls who'd been railroaded into 'performing' for charity. Saw one of them down a neat whisky. He flashed him a tight grin. Then Judith was back, telling him he was next up.

It wouldn't be the first time Blake had used his body like this. He'd sold out before. Women found him attractive, thought he was handsome. He'd been paid good money to trade his looks. He knew he was above the shallowness, the insincerity. Just keep it light. Think of the money—think of the charity. His time as a model all those years ago had taught him that women loved the brooding look. Not a problem. He really was brooding—on the revenge he'd have on his PA the minute she got back to work on Monday.

He listened to the words of introduction in disbelief. Judith, grinning at him from the opposite wings, had done a fine job in talking up his assets. He'd come up with some hideous filing task to keep her bored for hours on Monday. Then his name rang out and, with a deep breath and a muttered curse, he stormed onto the stage, automatically moving his feet in time to the beat of the loud music. Once he got to the centre he stopped, stood. Clenching his jaw, he stared out. The audience was semi-lit. He could see sparkle and lipstick and hair—everywhere. The blonde highlights dazzled. He carefully looked over the audience, happy to take his time. He walked closer to the edge of the stage, so he could window-shop as obviously as they were window-shopping him. Never show you were intimidated. He would at least pretend to be in control of this situation. Bluff through until he had them.

He caught sight of one particularly blinding blonde and sent her a small smile. The shrieks increased. He turned, walked in the other direction. Blow hot, blow cold. Women were fickle creatures. He knew how to keep them keen; he also knew not to trust them, certainly never to take them seriously.

But while his heart was permanently locked away from their clutches, his body didn't mind messing around now and then. The adrenalin kicked in, and he almost, almost, began to enjoy it. He winked at another screamer. Raise money, get the bids up, up, up.

He almost missed her, his eyes nearly passing over without seeing, except her stillness marked her out in the clapping, cheering crowd. She was the shadow to the blonde and bejeweled beside her. Her dark hair hung in a neat bob. Glossy and sleek, it enhanced her pale skin, ruby lips, the gentle curve of her cheek. She was staring at him. Not moving. Not talking. Not laughing or even nodding in time to the beat. Eerily still in the room full of chaos. He paused, for a second forgetting what he was supposed to be doing.

Stick-figure women dressed in black usually didn't do it for him. But this woman wasn't stick-thin and on her the black emphasized her creaminess—her full creaminess. His muscles tightened that little bit, a small flame sparking inside.

She wasn't shrieking, like the blonde next to her. She wasn't even smiling. But she was staring. A cool look that had him wanting to shake the reserve from her. He was seized with the desire to make her move. To make her sway, make her want, and above all he wanted to wipe that icy look of condescension from her face. She was judging. He was not a man to be judged. Not by her. Not in the negative way she so obviously was.

Blake liked his coffee strong and dark, a little bitter. He was looking right at a very tempting espresso. For, despite the lack of smile, despite the patent disapproval, there was fire in her eyes.

Double espresso.

The blonde beside her was grinning widely—at her rather than at him. She didn't seem to notice, she was too busy giving him that scornful look. For a long moment he stood as still as she sat. His jaw clenched, fists curled, and a wash of begrudging desire ran through him—desire to prove her wrong, to prove a point.

It became imperative not just to raise some money here, but some *serious* money. If he was going to sell himself, it would be for the highest price. At that he realized he'd better get back to the parading bit. For charity, he told himself, gritting his teeth and flashing a genuine tortured look.

He forced himself to relax, to smile at the harpy at the table on the other side, who had enough volume to drown out a crowd at a football match all by herself.

The experience from photographic shoots and catwalk struts came flooding back, his muscles remembering the way to move. With ease he prowled the length of the stage and back, pausing to deliver the 'look' now and then. He felt strangely energised, as if he were the one hunting out the prey, not the other way round. And he knew who his target would be this evening.

There was good-looking and there was ridiculous. The ripple of excitement through the audience had been obvious. Every eyebrow in the room had risen as that piece of perfection had so coolly moved out of the wings and onto centre stage with long, fluid strides and an insolent, daring look in his eyes. Edgy, angry man personified. And every woman in the room wanted to absorb his energy and take that dare head-on. Irresistible.

Cally wasn't unaffected. She sat, desperately keeping a grip on every one of her muscles, barely hearing the gushing sales talk of the MC so bowled over was she by *him*.

'Remember, ladies, he'll be your slave. Act on your every whim. Say the word and he'll deliver.'

Cally already knew he'd deliver. In that one moment when her gaze had locked with his he'd awakened a ferocious longing deep inside her. But then, she'd always had poor taste in men.

One woman at the table next to theirs shrieked so loudly Cally wondered for a second if the candle had somehow set the tablecloth on fire. But it was just him setting the entire bar alight. Hell, if he kept this up most of the women would be sliding off their seats. Cally knew she would if she hadn't crossed her legs over and clamped her inner thighs together, trying to deny the instant physical reaction in her body that had occurred simply from seeing him, for what, less than a minute? He was way too handsome. And he knew it. Totally knew it. Of course he'd deliver. He'd have the track record to prove it— the experience of two lifetimes probably.

Cally knew all too well that beautiful men had it too easy with beautiful women. Any woman. All women. And when men had it too easy, they played fast and loose and without care. Given how gorgeous this guy was, she had no doubt he'd be one hell of a jerk. But that didn't stop her body wanting to slither to the floor in a moist heap and scream 'take me'.

He'd turned towards the banshee at the table next to hers. His jaw clamped, eyes narrowed in cool appraisal. Then he deliberately let a slow smile spread across his features. Not a natural smile, not a genuine one. But one that emphasised his sensual lips and chiselled jaw and signalled the promise— carnal desire, sensual knowledge. He was playing it up for all he was worth, totally aware of his value and determined to leverage it.

Sexual awareness brewed with irritation in Cally. It was so typical that she should find a guy like this attractive. Brimming with sexuality and confidence, he'd be as promiscuous as she was celibate. Annoyance with herself—and him—made her temperature spike.

And then, of all the cheesy moves, he winked at the blonde banshee.

Cally let out a loud 'ugh' in disgust.

At that moment his gaze landed on her. His subtle smile disappeared, his jaw clamped, showing off to perfection his high cheekbones and strength. And the look of anger was genuine. He'd heard her. He'd seen her. And he was definitely unimpressed.

His gaze became a glare. Defiant, she glared right back. But then, in that infinitesimal pause, something flashed between them, something that pierced through their respective veneers. Cally saw through to a man who was simply doing someone a favour. And for one second she was sorry. She was not rude. His glare softened. What he had read in her, she didn't know. But she knew she felt damn uncomfortable.

Then he looked away, the MC kept advertising, and the strutting started again. Cally immediately told herself she had nothing to feel bad about. He was a first class performer, playing up to the ladies, standing in a way that emphasised his length and breadth. In order to even qualify as a bachelor for auction he had to have money, status. This guy had it all. And she hated him for it.

The auctioneer started the bidding. Cally was vaguely aware of the first bid, the auctioneer's fast-talking confidence. But mostly she was aware of the man on stage as he paced the length of it. And time and time again his glance collided with hers. He'd smile into the distance at some woman. Flash his brows at another. But when he intercepted her gaze, the smile was gone and there was nothing but challenge.

She could feel her body's response beneath her boring black dress. It must be some kind of basic instinct—that the female, when confronted with a tall, dark, ferocious-looking stranger, was overcome with the urge to know him in the most intimate way. It was as if her nether regions screamed 'fill me, give me your child'—the primal need for women to be attracted to the strongest, the fittest, the foreign. Genes like his were essential for the survival of the species and every female in the room knew it. Bitterness filled Cally as she registered his blatant virility. She couldn't have children. Not without a lot of help. And yet, she was still drawn to him, as if her body refused to believe its barren fate.

With just a look, a stance, he made woman want to lie and let him do as he pleased. And he'd please. That, more than anything, was the promise in his eyes.

Cally tried not to believe it. She wanted to look away. She really did. But it was impossible.

She was aware of movement beside her. At that she managed to turn and see Mel put up her hand, flutter her fingers.

'What are you doing?' Cally asked.

The blonde at the table alongside waved her arm wildly. So did two others across the room.

'Summoning the waiter.'

'Are you crazy? The auctioneer thinks you're bidding!'

'Oh.' Mel giggled. 'You got me.'

'You're kidding,' Cally tried to whisper while jealousy knotted in her tummy. So Mel thought he was hot too. And Mel was about to get married.

They were well into the thousands now—going up in blocks of five hundred. The auctioneer knew she was onto a winner.

Mel smiled serenely and waved again.

'I hate to break it to you, Mel, but you don't have that kind of money.' She pointed at the rock on her friend's fourth finger. 'When you get the band to match that, you'll have the money. But I really don't think this is what Simon would be wanting you to spend it on.'

'I'm not betting with my money. This isn't my bid.'

'Whose is it, then?'

Melissa turned to look at her, keeping her hand raised, flicking her fingers to show she was still in the game. 'Yours, silly.'

'What?'

'Come on, you wanted to donate to charity. And this is a good cause. A really good cause.'

'I don't need a bachelor for the weekend.'

'Your car needs a good clean.' She nodded to the front again.

'No, it doesn't.'

'Yes, it does.' Mel raised her hand higher. 'It needs a long, wet clean with lots of bubbles and a hunky, near-naked man bending over the bonnet.'

The mental image was enough to make Cally wish for an electric fan and a long cool drink. 'Stop this instant.'

'What are you going to do? Sack me?' Mel's grin was wide. She was clearly getting a kick out of the whole thing, and enjoying the evil looks she was getting from the blonde at the other table.

The bids went higher.

Cally didn't even know what his name was. She hadn't been listening when the MC had announced him. She'd been too busy helping herself to more of the truffles from that plate. Now she felt sick and the chocolates were all gone and she desperately needed more to cope with this.

'Mel…' wasn't listening.

The bidding went on, faster, higher, until suddenly it was all out war. Melissa versus the blonde at the table next door.

'Ladies, the competition is fierce here.' The auctioneer paused for breath.

Then he did it. Mr Eligible Bachelor sprang down from the stage and coolly walked to the two tables.

Panic rose in Cally as she saw even closer his height, his strength and the unmistakable fire in his eyes.

'Mel, stop.' She looked away from him and kept her eyes focused on the empty chocolate plate as if more would appear the harder she stared at it. 'If you don't stop, I'll get up and walk out and leave you with that huge bill.'

She had to stop her. On the one hand she felt totally intimidated, on the other hand she felt a rush of excitement unlike anything else.

'You'd never do that to me,' Mel breezed. 'You love me too much. Besides, the media is here.'

'What?' Cally turned her head, looking for the cameras.

Great, the last thing she needed was the world watching as she made a fool of herself.

The blonde at the opposite table was throwing them evil looks.

Melissa, with natural-born confidence, and the fact this wasn't her money, raised her hand again.

'Please stop, Mel.'

She couldn't explain why she felt so uncomfortable about buying someone's company. She'd never told Mel about Luc and she didn't have the time now. Anxiety twisted her tummy. She'd happily scoff another entire plate of truffles if she were alone. But she wasn't alone, she was in a roomful of shrieking women, out to buy men, and her best friend was buying one for her.

'Please, listen to me. I don't want him. Stop, OK?'

Mel, keeping her hand in the air, sent a sweet smile. 'Cally, honey, I'm doing this for you. I saw the look on your face when he walked onto the stage.'

'Don't be ridiculous.'

'He's hot. And, let's face it, Cally, you could do with some hot.'

Instead Cally iced over, and spoke slowly and clearly, her private school timbre carrying across the room. 'I do *not* need a gigolo.' She would never, ever *pay* someone to be in her company.

She finally chanced another look at the man Mel was so brazenly bidding for. He stood alarmingly close. Stock-still with his gaze locked onto her. His glance flickered between her and Mel and she knew he'd heard her last sentence. His eyes narrowed very slightly. Anger touched his features as his jaw tightened. Mel's arm was still up, ramrod-straight, right by her ear like the girly swot at school who knew the answer to the question before the teacher had even finished asking it.

She looked back at him and saw his attention was now wholly on her. She wanted to shrivel up and slither off behind a rock somewhere.

Then she heard the applause, the cheering. The blonde had retired from the race. The catch of the day was hers for the weekend.

'Fantastic!' Mel was practically frothing at the mouth, looking around for an official. 'Take the money. Take it. Take it.'

Stonily Cally reached into her bag, pulled out her pen and cheque-book. 'How much was he?'

'Does it matter? You have millions, Cally.'

Cally signed the cheque, then handed it to Mel to fill in the blank bits. 'Consider him a pre-wedding present. A last hurrah before you're bound into monogamy.'

'I'm already bound and well you know it.' Mel laughed. 'This one is all yours.'

'Not interested. I'm nipping away now. I'll talk to you tomorrow.'

'Cally…'

Happily one of the organisers swooped on Mel, animated and excited and thanking her for such a large bid.

Cally took the opportunity to escape. Clutching her bag, she rose from the table, then realised she was going to have to get past him somehow. And he wasn't budging. He stood, tall, silent, waiting by the table—waiting to wait on her. The butterflies in her tummy were beating their wings furiously and she fully regretted every single truffle. She turned quickly, stepping as fast as her short legs and stupid high heels would allow. As he refused to move and she refused to look at him, she had to brush past him, arm connecting with arm, hip connecting with hip. Goose-bumps spread over her skin and she quelled the shiver, striding out as fast as she was able.

She felt him turn back to Mel, but she blanked him from her mind, blanked the fire of the brief touch from his body. She headed to the exit.

Damn. The press hound from the society mag was striding towards her with purpose. Cally could only come up with the age-old escape—the bathroom. She'd had way more than enough excitement for the evening. If she waited a while in there the show would be back on with all eyes to the front and she could slip out the back unnoticed.

Inside the bathroom she hid out in a cubicle for a few moments until it sounded as if there was no one else in there. Then she went to the basin and washed her hands, running the cold water over her wrists to cool the blood racing in her veins.

Mel had only meant for her to have some fun, but she didn't know how hideous it had made Cally feel. She'd never forget the moment she'd found out about Luc—the hideous humiliation. Beautiful men weren't interested in Cally, not unless they were paid to be.

Cally closed her eyes against her reflection in the mirror. *Not going there.*

Instead she thought of her father. He'd been loving and warm and kind and had made the fact that her mother hadn't wanted her merely a niggle in her heart, not an aching tear. But he'd died and Cally had been left alone—and mother and daughter had been forced upon each other. Alicia the supermodel hadn't been prepared for the plump frump that had been her pre-pubescent daughter. Cally had tried, she'd really tried. But at five feet two she was never going to live up to her mother's five-foot-eleven grace and beauty and expectations. Under her roof, she'd been more alone than ever. And then there'd been Luc.

Cally frowned at the way her thoughts had come full circle. Then the music and noise coming from the bar increased in volume. The show was back on. Breathing a sigh of relief, she knew she could escape now. She pulled open the heavy door and walked out from the bathroom. And there, standing right in front of her, blocking her path, was her catch.

His hands rested on his lean hips, pushing his jacket back and revealing the white business shirt, emphasising the broad shoulders and the 'I'm in charge' air. What was it about men in suits? He looked authoritative, aggressive and ready for action. For a long moment he looked her up and down. She was doing the same to him but trying to be a whole lot more subtle about it, and as she tried not to slide into a heap she stiffened—standing straighter than a steel pipe.

Finally he spoke.

'When and where do you want me?'

CHAPTER TWO

NATURALLY 'here and now' was the first reply to spring to mind. Naturally Cally bit her tongue and looked anywhere but at him. She cleared her throat. 'I'm sorry?'

'This weekend. You. Me. What do you want me to do for you?' He was being deliberately provocative—surely?

She cleared her throat again. Got her larynx working. 'This was a mistake. My friend was doing the bidding. Yes, I paid the money, but you can go. Your weekend's free.'

'But I'm yours this weekend.'

She tried to smile politely but knew it was an abysmal effort. 'Look, that's really nice. But you don't have to take this that seriously. I just wanted to donate some money on the quiet, my friend thought it would be fun to bid. So.' She shrugged. 'There you go. You don't have to do the man-power bit.' She snuck a look at him then and immediately regretted it. Mr Tall, Dark and Determined stood over her and she was melting.

'She said you'd do this—try to get rid of me. She said I wasn't to let you and that if I wasn't with you for the weekend she'd tell the organisers and the money wouldn't go to charity.'

Cally rolled her eyes. 'As if they'd send my cheque back—they don't care what happens now. They have the money. That was the point.'

'I made a promise. I always deliver on my promises.'

Why wouldn't he go away? Why was he so insistent on

doing this when it had been so apparent she'd ticked him off? But then, maybe that was why. 'Look, if you have to do something, go and clean my friend's car.'

'She said she doesn't have a car and you know it. She said it's your car that needs a clean.'

Her irritation and discomfort started to leak through her fragile façade. 'I'm quite sure you've got better things to be doing with your time this weekend.' He'd have plenty of fish to fry—container-loads, in fact. Frustration forced her into unaccustomed rudeness—again. Without even a nod for goodbye she turned and started walking.

He didn't block her, rather kept pace every step of the way to the door, shielding her from the audience behind him.

'What are you doing?' she muttered.

'Sticking with you until you figure out my first task.'

She waited until they'd got outside and along the footpath away from the bar. 'This is ridiculous. You can go.'

'I never shirk my responsibilities.' He smiled then. One of those smiles designed to garner the acquiescence of anything and anyone in its path. But she also saw steel in his eyes. It didn't pay to look too hard into their sea-green depths. They'd have her saying yes faster than any of his other, many, draw cards. His determination to get her to say it, was palpable.

She stopped walking. Knowing she was never going to get rid of him until he'd won, she'd let him have this small victory. She opened her bag and found her pen and notebook. She wrote her address on it.

'Fine. Be here at nine tomorrow morning. You can wash my car.' Ultimately she'd be the winner. He could clean her car. But that was it.

He took the paper. Carefully folded it and put it in his breast pocket. His smile was small but satisfied. Genuine this time and more attractive than any he'd bestowed on the audience. 'Yes, ma'am.'

* * *

Blake pressed the buzzer right on eight fifty-eight a.m. The door opened in less than a minute. She wore loose linen trousers and a plain shirt and looked as if she'd been up for hours. On a Saturday morning you'd have thought a woman like this would be lying in and being loved. But he was stupidly glad she wasn't. He felt tight inside as adrenalin surged through him. Round one was about to begin. His desire to defrost this ice queen was motivation to win.

He watched her gaze skitter over him, saw pink lightly colour her pale cheeks.

She still wouldn't quite look up into his face. 'I'm sorry, I didn't catch your name last night.'

'Blake McKay.'

'Pleasure to meet you, Blake. I'm sorry if I was unappreciative of your determination to see this through. My name is Cally Sinclair.' Her automatic politeness irked him. It was so obvious she didn't particularly want him there, and yet she couldn't quite bring herself to say it. Ordinarily Blake preferred plain speaking. But he could play it her way for now.

'Enchanted, Cally.' He reached out and took her hand. The pleasure, at this point, was all his. But he was determined to have her appreciative in no time. The fact was, she fascinated him. He wanted to see her eyes go from disapproving to desirous. He wanted her to admit to the attraction that was making his heart race as he touched her.

She snatched her hand back. Not so politely. 'I've put my car on the drive for you. The garage is open. You'll find anything you need in there. Once you're done, you can go.'

Really? He had no intention of leaving after a half-hour car polish. What this stuck-up society miss needed was a good, hard—he pulled back his flare of anger.

'Damn expensive carwash.'

She ran another eye over his tee shirt and jeans. 'Feel free to hose off the drive after.'

The door shut in his face. So much for the polite act.

Little minx.

He knew she was attracted to him. Saw it in her eyes. But she was fighting it, denying it. Normally he couldn't care less. But he was attracted to her too. And more importantly she needed to be taught a lesson. She thought him a gigolo? Her words had burned, and brought back the memory of the time when he'd been used. He'd had no idea of the shallowness, the synthetic structure of Paola's world. He was quite certain Cally's world was equally shallow and not one he intended to hang out in for long. She was clearly spoilt and whether there was anything beneath that brittle society air he didn't know.

But he was going to find out.

He looked over her car. Blake, like many men, knew cars. And cars told a lot about their owners. This owner, he decided, was undoubtedly loaded. You'd need more than a few pennies to buy this baby. He checked the mileage—even more to buy it new as she most likely had. But it wasn't flashy. A stylish silver bullet. Not overly large but powerful within a sensuously curved form. Not unlike the lady owner herself.

She kept it well prepared, well organised, tidy. But she was also someone who liked comfort, who liked the feel of things. The state-of-the-art stereo, soft leather seats and the faint scent of berries hinted at someone who liked to employ all the senses.

He did the interior of the car first. It needed a clean as a cat needed a dog. But Blake was a perfectionist and as always he'd do a damn good job. And she had paid for it, after all. He found polish and leather cream and worked it over methodically, comprehensively, every last inch.

Forty minutes later it was time to do the exterior. He whipped his tee shirt off over his head to let the sun heat his skin. The inside of his body was already on fire. Burning resentment, desire, curiosity. He found the wax and rubbed it on, liking having the physical activity to burn off the energy her presence coiled in him. She was a little dynamo.

He heard the door slam and turned, hose in hand, to watch

as she headed towards him, her legs moving quickly. Her breath was coming short and fast, there was pink in her cheeks and her eyes sparkled.

'Can't you keep your shirt on?'

She fidgeted, still looking anywhere but at him. Her glance flicked to the surrounding houses. She was worried about what the neighbours would say? She looked to him finally and he'd have sworn the colour in her eyes deepened. Huge dark pupils stared up at him, surrounded by the rich dark coffee colour, and he wanted to drown in them. He blinked, broke the bond, and saw her cheeks were even pinker.

'No, it's hot out here.' He held the hose low, and flicked it a little so a jet of water splashed at her feet. 'Wanna get wet?'

Silence throbbed. For a beat or three she stared at him. Her mouth parted a fraction, then closed. Her lips pressed tight together. She turned away, her answer, when it came, more clipped than her high heels as they moved across the concrete. 'Certainly not.'

He called after her. 'May I get a drink?'

A pause in the staccato of the shoes. 'Of course.'

How anyone could deliver a reply with such finishing-school politeness and yet such defiance in her face, he didn't know. And damn if he didn't enjoy it.

Cally marched indoors wishing she could be rude enough to suggest he drink straight from the hose. She flustered her way to the kitchen. What to get the man? She was the one who needed long, cool and refreshing, not strong, hot and amazing. She needed a shower. Just past ten in the morning and she was more breathless and bothered than if she were attempting a circuit class at the gym.

Water, juice, lemonade?

Ice. Lots of ice. She turned to go to the freezer and there was nothing but bare, bronzed chest in front of her. She stared—at the defined abs, at the brown nipples, at the dusting of hair that arrowed down into the jeans, at the wall of heat before her. Oh, my. He'd followed her into the house and was up close. Very close.

'Like what you see?' Dry humour laced his tone.

She said nothing.

The pause grew. '*Want* what you see?' Less of the dry tone this time, a husky note of surprise.

Painfully wrenching her superglued eyes away, she stared at the glass in her hand and wondered what it was for.

Then she registered his questions—a good five seconds after he'd asked. Like? *Want?* Not able to answer honestly, she said the first thing that entered her head. 'I've made soup for lunch.'

There was another pause. Then, 'Why, thank you. I'd love some.'

Oh, hell. Had she just asked him to lunch with her?

'But water would be great for now.' He nodded to the empty glass in her hand.

The way she lost all thought compared to the confident way he handled himself was embarrassing. She walked round him to the fridge and challenged, 'You're so cool, aren't you?'

He grinned and leaned against the centre island bench. 'I guess. My nickname in my teens was cucumber.'

'You were that cool even at school?' She opened the fridge and leaned in, taking her time so the cold air might help her think straight.

'That might have been it or…' he answered lazily.

'Or what?' She poured water from the bottle, keeping the door open with her body.

'Maybe it was something to do with size…'

Size? The penny dropped. 'Ugh.' She slammed the fridge shut.

His laughter was low and dry and she sent him an evil look until he raised his hands in surrender. 'Kidding.' His laughter rumbled again as he looked at her still-fiery expression. 'Got you, though, haven't I?'

'Got me what?'

'Curious.'

She walked towards him. Deny, deny, deny—the heat in her body, the attraction to him. Maybe it was time she tipped the glass of ice and water over his way-too-hot body. It was like having a million-kilowatt heater in the room.

Eyes narrow and penetrating, he reached out and took the glass from her with a firm, steady hand. 'Careful.'

She raised her brows at him, not trusting her voice.

'If my jeans got that wet I'd have to take them off.' He took a long sip. 'And I'm not sure you're ready for me to take my jeans off yet.'

In that instant she knew she had to back off, right away. He was only fooling around but every word had her getting way too excited. He was so undeniably gorgeous, so cheekily charming, so *not* for her. No more mistakes.

But she was in her kitchen and he was in front of her face and there was nowhere for her to go. She tried to stand and stare him out—pretty hard when he had all the confidence, when he oozed the promise of satisfaction and she was overcome by the desire to test it out.

There was silence in the still kitchen. The teasing glint in his eye had gone and she watched the kaleidoscope of grey-green in his eyes, the widening of his pupils so that the colour was merely a thin outer ring and the centre was serious intensity.

It was a look that had her wanting all kinds of things—all of them involving getting closer. Instead she gave herself a mental kick in the butt. This was his stock in trade. He knew exactly what he was doing to her with his pattern of bold, daring comments, the laughter and cheeky half-apologetic grin and then the intense, searing stare. No way could any woman hold immune to it. She was drawn like the proverbial moth to the flame, and Cally still had scars from the last time she got singed.

But it was Blake who stepped away, breaking the stare, the burning light fading. Cally looked down to the bench. She fully regretted the soup invite, but good manners dictated she couldn't backtrack now. 'I'll call you when lunch is ready.'

'Sure.' She could feel his easy grin. 'I'll go finish out there.'

You do that, buster. She was going to keep her distance from now on. Cally focused on the chopping board as he turned to leave, but couldn't stop lifting her head again to appreciate the view as he exited the room. She could look, couldn't she? Especially when he wasn't watching. Especially at his butt.

When she called him back in Cally was initially relieved to note his shirt was back on. Unfortunately it was wet in patches and clung a little too tightly to his fit frame. She gripped the knife a little firmer.

'I'm done out there. You want to come and inspect?'

'No, I'm sure you've done a great job.'

She bent back to her task of chopping the herb garnish. He made himself right at home in her kitchen. Sending her a slight smile, he moved to inspect the pots simmering gently on the hob. He lifted the lid on one and sniffed.

'So this is the stuff you sell?'

She hid the surprise. So he'd done some homework between the auction and now. 'Sure. Gourmet soup. Made with the freshest and the best of ingredients, blended to perfection.'

'Smells good.' He turned the wooden spoon in another. 'And you make it all?'

'Why sound so surprised? You think I can't actually cook? You think I just add my name to someone else's recipe?' She'd done a degree in food science. She knew what was nutritionally valuable and what wasn't. And she loved experimenting with flavours and tastes. She'd taken the comfort eating thing and turned it into something positive. With a mother like Alicia, what choice did she have? She'd been put on that many diets.

He raised his brows. 'Did I say all that? Did I even suggest it?'

She felt faint warmth in her cheeks. 'It wouldn't be the first time someone implied that I've only used my connections to make a success of my business.'

'Well, I didn't imply anything of the sort. And from what I see here I can guess you make a success of your business all by yourself.'

She sent him a quick look of suspicion, but he didn't seem to be teasing so she gave him the humorous history that she didn't usually share. 'When I was a teen my mother decided a cabbage-soup diet would be the one to finally shed my puppy-fat.'

'Cabbage soup?'

She could hear his disgust and once she'd have totally agreed. She'd never hated her mother more than when she'd told her to detox for three days with nothing but some vile broth made from only onions and cabbages. She'd never felt so sick in her life. And so she'd gone into the kitchen, starving, and made her own soup. Then when her mother had grilled her on what she'd eaten that day she had been able to answer honestly—'just some soup'.

'I took to making it myself—played with the ingredients.' She'd added cheeses, meats, spices and flavourings to soup and turned something spartan and simple into something succulent and calorifically sinful. Her products had intense flavour, were highly sought after, and sold as soup for the connoisseur.

She moved to stand next to him at the hob, stirred the other pot and grinned at the recollections. 'Now my cabbage soup is one of my biggest sellers.' She looked up, forgetting that eye contact with him was dangerous to her mental agility. 'It has a full cup of cream in every pack.'

'Naughty Cally.'

She batted her lashes. 'What can I say? Subversive is sometimes the only way.'

'Subversive,' he echoed softly. 'I must bear that in mind.'

Staring up at him, she felt the heat from his gaze far more than the heat from the element that was threatening to burn the soup. Then, of all the ridiculous things, she shivered. Immediately his eyes darkened, and she sensed rather than saw his tiny movement closer and her own minuscule advance in response.

The rattle of the pot lid pulled her back. She turned the gas off quickly, lifted the pot and stepped away from his stifling nearness. Went back to mundane conversation. 'I make my own stock from scratch. I love the whole process.'

He watched her retreat with that teasing glint now back in his eyes. She knew damn well he knew how he affected her. He must be so used to it. But, man, it was humiliating. She told her backbone to lose the invisibility cloak. Couldn't she at least *try* to dish it out as well as him? Couldn't she tease him in the way he teased her? Meaningless, playful banter?

He stirred the soup in the other pot left on the hob with suspicion. 'Don't you ever eat anything else?'

She turned in surprise, then stopped to actually think about it. 'Not often, no.'

'You just live on soup?'

'Well, I have a smoothie for breakfast, then, yeah, soup for lunch and dinner. I'm usually in a hurry and just grab some from the shop. It's good to taste it—now that it's produced on a bigger scale I need to make sure none of the quality is lost.'

'Don't you ever want to chew on something? You don't get bored?'

'No.'

'Hmm.' He seemed to ponder for a moment. 'You know, I like something I can really get hold of. Something with some texture, some bite.' He looked back at her with wicked eyes again. She knew he was flirting, dangerously close to being bold. Well, she could handle that—couldn't she?

'Is that so?' She sent him a look from under her lashes, laughing inside at her pathetic attempt to inject cool into her voice. Then she turned to the fridge and opened the vegetable drawer that was always bursting with fresh produce.

The cucumber was thick and long and she weighed it with her hand, fingers curling tight around its girth as she turned back to him. She saw the sparkle in his eye and she gave him a bland smile back. The she picked up the biggest knife in her collection—not one she'd usually use on a hapless vegetable, but, in this instance, a point needed to be made. With quick, precise movements, she stripped its skin. She glanced back up to him. He'd stepped to the other side of her bench and was watching, the corners of his mouth twitching. She looked back down, slightly disconcerted, and got on with her dissection. Mr Cucumber could get a load of this.

For a few minutes the only sound was the bang, bang, bang as the blade hit the board. She worked swiftly, efficiently, until there was only a pile of pulp.

'So, let's see, you've skinned, deseeded and sliced that cucumber till it's barely recognisable.'

'Sure.' She had the cool tone down pat this time. 'I think we can safely say it's dead. Now it's ready to be eaten.'

'Only now that you've stripped it of its life force?'

'That's right.' She went back to the fridge and got the container of thick yoghurt. Spooned some into a dish, mixed it in with the cucumber and added seasonings.

'There are a couple to choose from, but I think you should try the spicy sausage.' She spoke over her shoulder as she spooned the steaming soup into a bowl. 'I think you'll find it has plenty of texture and bite. You may even need some of the yoghurt dip to take the edge off.'

'The one with the cucumber? Because, let's face it, without the cucumber, that dip would be nothing.' He grinned then. It widened into a full-blown smile and laughter followed. Warm, rich, irresistible laughter. Suddenly, effortlessly, Cally found laughter bubbling out too.

'You're not all you seem, Cally,' he teased as their humour dimmed.

'In what way?'

'There's a little more to you than I expected.'

'What did you expect?'

'As little as you expected from me, I think.'

She looked up quickly, only to be caught again by his gaze.

'Not just a pretty face,' he murmured.

She got back to fussing with the bowls pronto. He wasn't talking about her. She wasn't a pretty face at all; she was plain and ordinary. And his face wasn't pretty either; it was beautiful. 'Never go out with a man who is better looking than you'— that was her motto. She just had to remember to stick to it.

'You mind eating in here? The formal dining room doesn't get the sun at this time of day and it seems a shame not to make the most of it.' She set the bowls at the stretch of bench along the window.

'No problem. This looks great.'

He waited politely until she'd placed her own bowl and was seated alongside him. She gestured to the condiments, and the fresh chopped herbs. 'Please.'

'Thank you.'

They dipped their spoons together and she watched as he lifted his to his mouth. She barely tasted her own soup as she was so focused on seeing his reaction.

He took a moment, then smiled. 'It's good.'

CHAPTER THREE

CALLY felt more pleased than if she'd won the gold medal at the annual gourmet food awards. To cover it, she schooled her features back to bland and murmured, 'I know.'

She took another mouthful before offering a polite query, all the while refusing to acknowledge the knowing smile of amusement on his face. 'What do you do, Blake?'

'Do?'

'Yes, as in job.'

He looked surprised. 'I'm a venture capitalist.'

'Really? Who with?'

The surprised look broadened. 'I have my own company... Weren't you listening to the intro the MC gave me last night?'

She shook her head. 'I was too busy eating the chocolate truffles at the time.'

'Priorities.' Full of satire, his smile twitched.

'Absolutely.' In contrast she spoke earnestly. 'I never intended to bid. That wasn't why I was there.'

He didn't reply and she wondered if he didn't believe her or if it was just that he was too busy demolishing the soup. It didn't take either of them long. Good. She stood to clear the bowls, hoping soon she'd be rid of him—she needed to work on her resistance.

'Thanks very much—that was delicious.' He stood, stretched, his body towering over her.

'It was a pleasure,' she answered mechanically. He was too close again and the tremors inside could hardly be controlled. 'I don't have any more jobs for you. So thank you very much and…um…I'll see you out.'

'I don't think so, Cally.'

She'd feel intimidated if she didn't feel so turned on. She stared as he walked closer towards her.

'I don't think I should leave yet.'

'As I said, I don't have any other jobs…'

'I wasn't thinking about doing any more jobs.' He cocked his head to the side, looked a little too sexy. 'I was thinking we should talk some more.'

'What about?'

'Us. This…' he made a juggling gesture with his hands '…*zing* between us.'

'Zing?' Her voice leapt up an octave or three.

He moved closer. 'You want me. I can see it.' He stepped again so they were almost touching and she tensed even more. 'You jump every time I come near you.'

'Um.' How did she answer that one? Her cheeks alone were telling him everything he needed to know—that he was right.

'I want you. You want me. It's simple.'

She knew it was pointless to even try to deny it. The tension in her muscles increased and yet at the same time her insides were melting—he wanted her? She shook her head free of the fantasy. This was just some game—he was just acting the bachelor auction part.

'It's not simple. And my wanting you is stupid.'

For a second satisfaction flashed across his face. She had a weird blip of pleasure in seeing that her admission pleased him.

'Why?'

'You're not my type.'

'I'm not?' He looked disbelieving.

It made her all the more determined. Coldly she reinforced her reply. 'Not at all.'

She turned on her heel, went to the sink and started rinsing dishes.

At a far more leisurely pace he followed, coming to stand too close, again. And his questions were too close too. 'When did you last get any? You're looking way too uptight.'

Astounded, she turned. 'You are sailing dangerously close to the wind.'

'Hmm. I like a little dangerous.'

She let her look say it all. Only he seemed to find it amusing rather than quelling. He leaned across, his hand trapping hers on the tap as he spoke low and tauntingly in her ear.

'You know what you need? You need a good hard—'

She yanked her hand out from under his. 'Don't say it. Don't you dare say it.'

'What was I going to say?' He looked all innocence again—the devilish rake disappearing in a disarming smile.

'It's time you were leaving. My lover is due here any minute and he's the jealous type.'

'Liar.' He laughed. 'No jealous lover would let you loose at a man auction. No lover would leave you alone on a Saturday morning.'

'Fine. No lover—jealous or otherwise. It's still time you were leaving.'

'No, it's not.'

'You are so confident, aren't you?' she snarled. 'It's a wonder your bed still stands with all the notches you've carved into all four legs.'

'Why are you so determined to think me some sort of Don Juan?'

'Well, aren't you? Have you listened to yourself recently?'

He chuckled, acknowledging the hit. 'I don't usually talk quite like this, Cally. It's just that you make it impossible not to.'

'Yeah, right.'

'Look, I like to keep in shape, but I'm not the sleazy playboy you seem to think I am.'

'Keep in shape? It's a form of exercise for you?'

He gave an outrageous grin. 'Sometimes. It can be a wonderful stress relief, you know.'

'Hasn't anyone made it difficult for you?'

'Not recently.' He sighed. 'OK, so I've had some fun in my past, but I don't want some image-obsessed bimbo—a vacuous body too concerned with the pose she's in to be able to give as good as she gets. That actually gets pretty boring after a while.'

'To be able to give as good as she gets?' Cally was stunned at his arrogance. 'You really think you're that good?'

'No. But I always put my all into it and sometimes the chemistry…you can't contain an explosion. But that kind of chemistry is rare.' He paused. '*This* kind of chemistry.' He inched closer, voice dropping. 'I'm only interested in this kind of chemistry now and I haven't encountered it in a long time.'

'So, what, you're telling me you're celibate?'

'Not entirely.' He cleared his throat. 'But I'm guessing you are.' His eyes twinkled. 'And you shouldn't be.'

She turned back to the sink. 'It all comes too easy for you.'

'Why not have some fun, Cally?'

She wanted to bury her head in her hands. But it was strangely fascinating, liberating, to tackle it head-on.

'When did you last have an orgasm?' He sounded as if it were the most natural thing in the world to ask.

She winced. Head on was right. She couldn't believe she was leaning against her kitchen sink in the early afternoon with an almost stranger analysing her sex life.

The last time she had an orgasm? How did she answer that?

Cally was used to being in the minority for lots of things: in the small fraction of female entrepreneurs; the twelve per cent of the world's population that was left-handed; well shorter than average; one of the few unfortunate enough to have a faded supermodel for a mother…and part of the small percentage of women who'd never had an orgasm during penetrative sex.

Truth be told, Cally had never had an orgasm in any kind of sex. She'd faked it. Took her inspiration from the movies. It wasn't that she was left cold. It was just that she'd never quite got there. She'd got close with Luc. She had. But he'd never taken the time. It had always been over just as she'd been getting warmed up.

Of course, once she'd found out, she'd known he'd just been getting it over with. They'd only slept together a dozen or so times. A few weeks when she'd thought she was madly in love, and he'd been doing her mother a favour. Not even a favour—doing a job. Paid for and everything.

She hadn't tried much since. She'd kissed, and got to whatever base it was that was almost all the way there. But old insecurities were hard to let go of—that she wasn't really attractive, that men were only interested in her because of her connections or her wealth. And once she found out the extent to which her endometriosis had hindered her chances of a family she knew she didn't have much to offer a man.

So Cally had decided she didn't need a guy, didn't need sex. She could be single and celibate and have a fabulous life—especially with her career. Most of the time she didn't even think about it. The ability to trust men had been beaten out of her. Since Luc she'd embraced the 'why bother' approach wholeheartedly. And most of the time she was happy. She focused on her business, and smoothed over the scar on her heart that said husband and kids weren't for her. That was fate. She didn't need the grief of worrying about it any more. You didn't miss what you'd never had—right?

But then, occasionally, there were wants. And Blake McKay was all want for her.

'I'm serious. When did you last have an all-body, all-screaming release?'

'I'm not discussing that with you.' In the split second after she'd answered the question every single doubt reared in her head and every single reason why she was single stood in her brain, itemised in a flashing neon bullet-pointed list. And, despite years of happily getting over it, getting on with it, it hurt.

'You can't even say it, can you?'

'Orgasm!' she shouted. 'Orgasm, orgasm, orgasm, orgasm!' She glared. 'Satisfied?'

'Not nearly.' His grin was wide and wicked. 'Five.' He nodded. 'Five times. Five times in one night.'

She looked at him blankly.

'Is what I promise you.'

'You're kidding. Five in one night?' Transfixed, she gazed at him. 'You really think you could?'

'Like I say. Chemistry. Inevitable explosion.'

So she was tempted—and he knew it. For one mad moment she considered it—a wild fling. Five big Os in one night— could he really? Was it even possible? Hell, if anyone could, he could. He might deny it but a playboy he was—experienced. And if nothing else mattered, if nothing was at stake— most definitely not her heart—could she be free long enough for it to happen? Hell, she didn't need five, one would be enough.

'No one ever has to know.'

She bit hard on her lip to hold back the groan that had its origins in her belly.

He leaned into her, and she stared into the stormy sea eyes. 'Why wouldn't you act on an attraction this strong?'

She sucked in air, and refused to let herself think he was as attracted to her as she was to him. This was some sort of game. He was so used to winning and he only wanted to have her because he thought he could—she didn't want to be just another milestone on his way.

He reached out, ran his knuckles down her cheek. 'This can't be faked.'

Her face flamed under his touch, her lips desperately dry.

'You can't fake it with me, Cally.'

Her knees were at risk of failing and she was about to crumple to the floor. If she turned her head just a fraction those fingers would brush her lips. Blood buzzed to them; she wanted to feel him...

Injection of steel required immediately! Memories of Luc burst into her brain. She'd believed a pretty face and some pretty lines before and been so burned she'd never trust another. She walked away from Blake, put the island between them again, chewing away the tingling sensation in her lips as her back was turned to him.

But she had to admit she liked his blunt approach, his un-ashamed candour. At least he seemed to be up front—again it was liberating. And she'd return the favour.

She turned to face him, put her hands on the bench, sighed deeply. 'Don't take this the wrong way, but you're actually too good-looking.'

'I'm sorry?' He leaned against the opposite side of the bench, bending so their faces were level.

'Yes, you know. Thick dark hair. Big green eyes. Long lashes. Square jaw. Stubble. That's just your face. I'm not even starting on your body. I'm not going any lower than your chin.'

The smile broke his intense expression, lit him up from the inside. 'I'm too good-looking for you to have fun with?'

'Yes.'

He laughed. 'So you only go out with ugly guys?'

She was silent.

'I begin to see why it is you've been without for a while.' He leaned closer, spoke to her slowly as if English were a foreign language to her. 'You know there's a big flaw in your argument. You have to be attracted to the person. If you think he's ugly he isn't going to turn you on, sweetheart. What are you going to do—lie back and think of England?'

'History has proven that I have terrible judgment, terrible taste in men.'

'Based on looks?'

She nodded. 'I get bamboozled by them. Blinded, can't determine the false from the genuine.'

He frowned. 'You can't see past the exterior to work out whether inside the person is OK or not?'

'No.'

'So now if he's good-looking, he's immediately a no-go?'

Reluctantly she smiled at his bemusement.

'But physical attraction is a pretty major ingredient, isn't it?' He wasn't dropping it.

'Sure it is. But it's not just me who thinks you're good-looking. Look at the battle at the auction last night. Women were beside themselves over you—practically launching at you from the aisles.'

'*You* weren't. You didn't even want my services and you'd paid for them.'

She grimaced. 'My friend bought you. She just used my money because she knew I, along with the rest of them, thought you were attractive.'

'So what if others find me attractive?'

'I could never trust you. And I could never trust other women around you.'

Blake stood, head tilted as he considered her reply. He watched the rush of honesty reflected in her face and saw that the brown in her eyes was starting to melt. 'Do you take everything so seriously? Who needs trust? We're talking a bit of fun, not marriage and babies. I never talk marriage and babies.'

Not any more. Not ever. It was important she understand that. Paola had taken him for a ride once long ago and it was a ride he'd never take again. It still hurt so much he could hardly breathe when he thought of it. The way he'd been so vulnerable, how badly he'd wanted exactly those things— marriage, their baby. But she hadn't, and she had got rid of both him and their baby. He sucked in a quick breath, pushed the pain away. Instead he concentrated on the temporary temptation before him, with her gaze that told of provocation but also barely hidden interest.

'Why am I not surprised?'

She was determined to peg him as a philanderer—trying to use it as a flimsy barrier against the red-hot attraction that was pulling them together. He, conversely, didn't see the point in fighting it. If they gave in to it, it would wane and disappear. One night full of passion would do the job nicely.

So she'd been messed about by some pretty boy some time and was shoehorning him into the same mould. Did what she thought of him really matter? Oddly it did. He'd been above angry at the auction, seeing the contempt so clear on her face. He wanted to prove her wrong.

And he couldn't stop the attraction that was making him step beyond boundaries, the pleasure in seeing her cheeks flush as their conversation veered into the deeply personal. He wanted to know her, inside and out—but he had to establish the ground rules first. He'd make sure she understood exactly what it was between them—transient lust and nothing more. Then they'd be free to indulge it—and he would make sure she was more than satisfied. Equal participants aiming for extreme pleasure.

'So how long has it been?'

He watched her expression as irritation warred with uncertainty. She didn't reply. Clearly it had been quite some time. Wholly chauvinistic satisfaction washed through him. Good. He didn't like the idea of other men holding her.

'OK. So you're unimpressed by my looks. I'll have to win you with my other charms, won't I?' She'd surprised him, admitting to her attraction like that. But she'd also made it clear she wasn't going to act on it—which irritated him no end. Not only because he wanted her to, but because fundamentally he was a man of action. When you saw something that needed doing, you did it.

And Cally Sinclair needed doing.

If they could have a weekend of good, hard, physical fun they could walk away and no one be any the wiser—a consideration he sensed was important for her and one he was happy to allow. He just wanted to see her face pink from pleasure, her eyes drowsy, wanted to feel her shudder around him, wanted to see her relaxed in the way that only sex could make you relaxed. He wanted to watch her the moment that sensation overruled mind—at her most basic, where manners and social niceties were long abandoned and need was driving her. Need for him. And, yes, he wanted her in a state where she'd do anything for him. Panting, pleading, begging. The way she'd dismissed him still rankled—so he was a gigolo that she didn't need? Well, he'd see about that. He planned to drive her crazy, to have her admit her desire for him—not just with her mouth but with her body, to have her unable to deny it. He wanted to shake this prim little bird from its tree and watch it fly. He was certain she would soar.

Determination marked her features as she shook her head. 'Not going to happen. I've told you, you're not my type.'

'I think you're clinging a little too tight to that line.'

'You've way too much ego for me.'

He stared at her for an explanation. Grumpily she gave him the angle he'd hoped for.

'Come on, the way you were parading up on that stage...'

'It was for charity,' he answered easily before starting to dig. 'Anyway, you were the one handing over the money. You bought me. Paying for a bloke?'

'It was for charity.' She was ultra-defensive; her mouth tightened. 'It wasn't about the result, the prize—about you—it was about fundraising for people less fortunate than ourselves.'

'Really? My, what a philanthropist. Well, what are you willing to *do* for charity, Cally? How far would you go?'

'I give a lot to the causes I believe in.'

'Bully for you. Hell, it must be hard getting together with a bunch of girlfriends for a boozy night ogling men in the name of charity. Sitting there thinking of all those poor people as you eat your chocolates and drink your champagne and decide which hunk you want to clean your car. That's really doing your bit, Cally.'

He'd crossed the line now, and damn if he wasn't enjoying every minute of it. Time to make a play for it. 'I have a suggestion for you.'

She barely registered interest, she was too busy looking annoyed.

'Let's have a competition. Our own little thing for charity. We each start Monday morning with, say, a hundred dollars in the kitty. We fundraise. For a week. At the end of the week whoever has raised the most wins.'

'Wins what?' Curious now, fixed on him.

'If you win, I'll double the combined amounts and give it to the charity of your choice.'

'And if you win?' Her eyes were wide.

'If I win then I get you for a weekend and can do whatever I want with you.'

'Whatever you want?' She sounded as breathless as if she'd climbed a thousand stairs.

'You'll be my slave.'

Cally gulped in a deep breath. And another. 'You're kidding, right?'

'No.' He smiled but searched with his eyes. 'Not keen? You wouldn't go far for your charity, would you? All talk. See, I was quite happy to give my time. You're only willing to give your money.'

'That's not true.' Indignation burned as she thought of the hours she'd spent at the shelter. But she wasn't about to tell him what she did every Thursday night—and had done since she was a child. Her father had taken her, week in, week out, to stand in the kitchen and help prepare the meal. It was his way of showing her that not everyone lived in mansions with more servants than residents. And if you were fortunate enough to be born into a position in which you had both time and resource to help others, then you gave both time and resource. It was a lesson she'd embraced—never wanting to have the shallow lifestyle of her mother. Wanting to give back, wanting to be more her father's daughter than her mother's. She'd been going there so long she had a close bond with many of the long-term drop-ins, and had shared much with the other volunteers and the manager. It was just her small way of making a difference. Quite often it was the highlight of her week and she'd never abandon them.

So she didn't need to prove anything to Blake McKay, did she? He could think what he liked. And as for what he was suggesting? No way.

She refused to acknowledge the imp in her head that was screaming 'go for it'. 'There's a bit of a difference between cleaning a car and what you're…implying.'

He looked amused. 'I wouldn't be doing anything that you didn't agree to.'

'I wouldn't agree to anything like that.'

'Then you've nothing to worry about, have you?' His grin widened.

OK, so *now* she felt the need to prove something to him. That he wasn't going to have it all his own way, all so easily. Not with her. She'd definitely be the one to get away. 'Anyway, it's more than likely I'll raise more money than you.'

'Indeed. All those wealthy friends you have. Make a few calls and you'll have a few thousand just like that.'

Oh, he thought she'd do that, did he? Her eyes narrowed. 'I don't beg from my friends. They have enough obligations. When I fundraise I do it properly.'

'I'm sure you do everything properly, Cally.'

The implied criticism was too much. 'Fine. You're on. One hundred, starting Monday. Shake hands to seal the bet.' She held hers out across the bench, primly, a little high.

He ignored it. 'No. A kiss to seal the bet.'

'Fine.' She'd show him immune—starting right now.

She watched warily as he walked around the island, turning with him so the bench was at her back and he was in front of her. He stepped so close she didn't think she had room to breathe. One arm came either side of her and he rested his hands on the bench, totally hemming her in—strong barriers, and an even stronger set to his jaw.

Oh, dear. Her immunity was fast disappearing. She didn't know what to do with her hands, didn't want to reach out to him, so she tucked them behind her back and clutched at the curved edge of the stainless steel bench. Bad move, because it meant her entire torso—and below—was exposed and pushed slightly in his direction. If he leaned just a fraction closer they'd have full-body, length-to-length contact. Her breathing shortened. Could he hear her heart?

A mocking smile touched his features. 'You'd better close your eyes.'

He was right. Because this close his looks were searing into her and her blood was thudding through her body. She felt hotter than if she'd been grilled on high in her top-of-the-range European oven.

He took his time watching her as she struggled to decide what to do. Why couldn't her brain work? This was ridiculous—what had she just agreed to?

'Close them.' A soft command.

Her lids fluttered. It was easier to obey. But her mouth opened—to argue, right? To get in some air? Not because she wanted to let him in.

Yeah, right.

It was a moment before he made contact, a moment in which she fought to restrain her body from meeting his. Because frankly her lips were on fire and if he didn't touch his to them soon she couldn't be responsible for her actions. Her reason, her rationality, seemed to have gone on an extended lunchbreak.

But Blake didn't take what she was offering, not in the way she wanted. He didn't plunder and ravage, didn't press his mouth hard on hers even though she half longed for a kiss that demanded everything, that simply took right from the start. Instead he touched her gently. The contact was slow and almost annoyingly sweet. His lips over hers were firm and warm and he tasted, damn him, of a hint of cucumber—all cool and in control.

Then the sweetness became less annoying, more intoxicating and more inviting. She squeezed her fingers harder on the cold steel of the bench—not going to reach for him. Not going to.

She couldn't help her tongue, though, from seeking out his depth and the essence, teasing him all by itself. And suddenly the kiss changed and his plunder element surfaced. Satisfaction coursed through her as the pressure increased, as did the demands—for both of them. His Saturday morning stubble rasped on her soft skin and she wanted to feel more of his hair roughened body against her—like all of it, now. With a barely audible moan she opened more to him and he leaned closer to take full advantage, going deeper, lusher. Still not close enough, not for Cally. Finally his lips left hers and she felt his breath hot and fast on her face and she doubted the degree to which he was cool and in control.

She felt the space between them grow as he quickly pulled away.

'A very willing little slave.'

His confident drawl hit her. He was the boss, huh? She didn't think so, not from the way he was gulping in the air. Slowly she raised her lashes and looked at him as coolly as she could. 'Just who do you think was the slave then?'

His brows lifted. 'Did I say five? I think we'll make it six. Let's really prove that exact point.'

He'd almost exited the room and she'd almost slid to the floor to assume the recovery position when he stopped. Turning back to her, he spoke, no hint of a grin, just the edgy, angry model-man look.

'I should warn you. I never make promises I can't keep.'

CHAPTER FOUR

FIRST thing Monday morning there was an email.

> 9 a.m. Monday, one hundred dollars. 5 p.m. Friday, let me know your total. You know the prize.

Cally did and she also knew she didn't have a snowball's chance in hell of beating him at this game. Sixth sense told her no matter how she played it he'd go one better—as he had every step of the way so far. She'd run a Google search on him two seconds after reading the email, and looked at only the first few hits of the many that came up—the bio on his company website, plus a few articles in which he was portrayed as a major mover and shaker in the business world. Hell, she'd had no idea; all she knew was soup. How insulting had she been? He knew how to make money—serious money—and, while Cally had serious money, she wasn't so good at making more. Sure, her company did OK, but it was niche and she knew if she really wanted to expand she needed leverage and expert advice. But she wasn't sure expansion was the way to go. It would be nice to keep it the size it was—even though she could hardly keep up with it. She worked round the clock, seven days, and still couldn't seem to keep on top of it all. Her beloved time experimenting in the kitchen was suffering major erosion.

And now, instead of getting on with the job, she turned her

back on the overflowing in-trays and panicked about their stupid competition some more. It was hardly sausage-sizzle and cake-stall stuff. She had no time to organise anything. Fundraising did not mean asking her wealthiest buddies for a handout—anyway, how could she possibly explain the real reason behind it? And what could she 'do' to raise sponsorship? Again there was no time and, as far as she was aware, there weren't any marathons being run between now and Friday. Not that she'd manage even half a mile…

Besides, if she was honest, did she really want to win? Didn't she want to win in the best way possible—to be there for the weekend and not give in to him?

That one was a fantasy—seriously delusional and she knew it. Just the memory of that kiss—the one that had been on auto-replay ever since, despite her best 'delete' efforts—had her burning up to such a degree it was a wonder she was still whole and not some speck of cinder being blown on the breeze. It would take less than a second of contact and she'd be his.

So, she'd better win the competition because she *refused* to be another easy conquest for him. The only hope she had was her business. She went down to Mel in the shop at the front of the small factory where she had five workers making the soup.

'Every pottle we sell this week we donate fifty cents to charity.' She worked up a sign. Put it in the window. Put a jar beside the cash register alongside the tip jar for the staff.

'Are you sure?' Mel looked sideways at her. Already Cally's Cuisine donated a percentage of profit to charity. Cally could understand the question.

'Yes. I need to really raise some funds for this charity. It's important. Just this week—a one-off fundraiser.'

'What charity?'

The 'save Cally from utter humiliation' charity—not that she told Mel that. 'The usual.'

Mel had lost interest in the topic anyway, had a cunning smile on. 'How was your weekend?'

Cally had been putting off this moment for as long as possible by hiding out upstairs and pretending to be super busy and not up for chat. 'He cleaned my car and then left.' As crisp and matter-of-fact in delivery as she could manage.

It was enough. Mel shook her head. 'You're a lost cause.'

'Ain't that the truth,' muttered Cally.

Wednesday afternoon she worked in the shop to cover Mel's break. Panic was definitely setting in. She rattled the jar on the counter; a few coins clinked together. The weather was warm and sales were down. Why couldn't there be a wintry blast and soup be the dream diet of everyone?

She was just packing an order when another customer walked in. She looked up, her sales smile in place, and froze. He stood, wearing an immaculate suit and a devilish glint in his eyes. She fumbled her way through seeing off the other customer, all thumbs and heated cheeks, fully resenting the grossly unfair way he'd been given such perfect features—all of them.

He nodded towards her sign. 'How's the fundraising going?'

'OK. You?'

'Not bad.' He flashed a smile she didn't like. 'I'll take some of that cabbage one.'

She put a pack in the bag, gave it to him and assumed cool composure. 'On the house.'

He inclined his head in thanks and then put his hand in his pocket, withdrawing his wallet anyway. With relaxed style he took out a note and stuffed it into the charity box. A hundred-dollar bill, no less.

Cally looked at him. 'Not bad, huh?'

He winked and left the shop. Cocky was not the word. It cemented the knowledge that, come what may, he was going to win—through sheer determination. The same way, she suddenly realised, that he'd been determined that she win him in the auction. He had that same look—challenging her, daring her.

She went straight upstairs and phoned her regular beautician. Late Thursday afternoon she left the salon after three hours locked inside. She was smooth, soft and totally depressed. Her bob sat sharp and gleaming, her toenails were trimmed and polished and every bit in the middle had been tended to and buffed. She was still depressed. She amended the sign in the shop and called to Mel.

'Every soup we sell we donate three dollars to charity.'

'Cally, that means we're running a loss.'

'I don't care.' She looked at her concerned employee. 'Oh. OK. I do care. Two dollars.'

'You're the boss.' Mel shrugged. 'I know there's something more going on here.' A coy look. 'Your hair looks nice.'

Cally hated her hair. There was nothing to be done with it. Thick, dead straight and as brunette as you could get. She'd tried over the years—but when you spent seven hours getting highlights that you had to then hunt for under interrogation-style lighting, well, you knew it was a lost cause. So every few weeks she had it cut into a razor-sharp bob and ignored it the rest of the time. She'd never be blonde. She'd never be particularly beautiful. She was brunette, short and most definitely veering to round. Spending an afternoon surrounded by blonde glamazons—and that was the beauticians, she wasn't even thinking about the other show-stopping clients—was not good for Cally's self-confidence.

She drew a deep breath and told herself, not for the first time, to get over it. She checked her watch. She was due at the shelter in less than twenty minutes. Her step lightened. This was just what she needed. Some time doing something for someone else, far worse off than her, would put her own silly worries well into perspective…till tomorrow anyway.

The next evening he called to her as she approached. It was the bar where the auction had been held. Had he deliberately chosen the table where she'd sat last week? She knew he had. She was fast learning that nothing about Blake wasn't deliberate.

'Had a good week, Cally?'

'Not bad.' Cautious. 'You?'

'Not bad.' He watched as she sat, then flicked his fingers for a waitress.

Cally's sense of trepidation increased. 'Vodka martini, please,' she ordered, hoping the bartender would pour with a heavy hand and spare the mixer.

Finally she summoned the nerve to ask him. 'How much did you raise?'

He held up the paper in front of him. Cally looked at the figures—all five of them, and that was before the decimal point. She didn't know whether she was about to laugh hysterically or burst into tears.

'How?'

'I invested my one hundred dollars.'

'And you made that much in a week?' Hell, she should be talking to her financial planner; he wasn't doing nearly well enough if Blake could get that sort of return in only a week.

He grinned. 'High-risk investments. All or nothing. I got lucky.' He put the paper down and pushed it towards her. 'It was worth the risk. I wanted to win.' He gestured to more paper poking out of his laptop bag. 'I can show you a record of the transactions if you'd like.'

'No. I believe you.' She took a quick sip of the dry drink. 'How badly did you want to win?'

'As badly as you wanted me to.'

Her eyes closed for a second.

He spoke again, still in that low voice that made her want to move nearer to him, to hear what else he might have to say, to feel his breath on her face, to sense his heat. She could feel it even now.

'Are you going to tell me you didn't want me to win?'

She couldn't lie. Avoidance was the best option. She opened her eyes and stared straight into his, a whole lot closer than she'd expected and luminous green. 'Where and when do you want me?'

CHAPTER FIVE

BLAKE had surprised Cally with the where. She'd anticipated some luxury pad in the centre of the city—a penthouse apartment with all the mod cons and restaurants on the ground floor or some such. But he'd given her a beach address a short drive out of the city. As soon as she'd got the time and place from him in the bar she'd knocked back her drink and skedaddled out of there. She'd imagined, morosely, he'd probably gone on to score. She'd seen a trio of women less than subtly eyeing him up even when she'd been sitting beside him and all his attention had been on her.

She frowned, trying to analyse him as she drove to his address. What was his interest? Why was he so keen to 'win' her?

He had wealth of his own so he wasn't a fortune hunter. He definitely wasn't desperate for dates. Yet he had fixed his sights on her. Probably, she decided, because she was that challenge—she'd said no right from the start and no wasn't an answer he liked.

She should have the strength to keep saying no—it would do him good to fail for once. But what he offered was getting way too hard to resist. She couldn't offer anyone marriage and children, and he admitted he didn't want either. Why not simply take advantage of a skilled lover? Have the experience she'd never had. And, as he'd pointed out, no one would ever know.

But there was that part of her that resented giving him his way. He'd had his way too much, for too long. It was evident in the arrogance stamped on him. She sighed. The least she could do was to try to keep this on her terms.

The gates were open and she drove straight up the drive and to the house at the top.

It was large. And incredibly beautiful. She breathed deeply, certain the air was fresher here than even only fifty kilometres down the road.

He opened the door even before she'd had the chance to lift her finger from the buzzer.

His eyes raked down her. Her shirt—that she'd buttoned up to the top—might as well be invisible the way he seemed to look right through it.

'You came.'

The faint surprise in his tone surprised her. 'Well, not yet. Isn't that why I'm here?'

His grin glowed with delight. 'Was that humour from you? Did you just crack a joke?'

Coolly she walked past him and into his house. She was not going to show the extent to which she had the shakes. Why did he have to look so damn irresistible in jeans and a tee? It was very difficult not to walk right up to him and pounce. So much for saying 'no'—one glance and it was all over.

To pull back her raging lust she focused on finding out her tasks—assuming he'd thought of something.

'Where did you want me to start? I'm good in the kitchen, as you know. Must admit I'm not so great with a mop, but I can handle a vacuum cleaner—'

'Cally, you are not going to be doing my housework.'

'No? No odd jobs for me to do? I can make some soup.' She looked about as if a sign labelled 'kitchen' would miraculously appear. The room was light and airy. Neutrals—white, fawn. Light and clean, and the view out to the ocean was spectacular.

'Lunch is already taken care of. I have other plans for you. You're my entertainment for the weekend.'

'Entertainment?' She kept looking about, too jumpy to tackle him visually. She might tackle him literally. Somehow she wanted to work a little, just a little, dignity into this situation.

'Yeah. Are you any good at belly dancing? I've a feeling you'd look wonderful in one of those costumes.'

At that she looked at him, and saw the lazy amusement. It sparked a minor rebellion. 'Damn, I left my dress-up box behind.'

'Shame.' He glanced at the gauzy curtains. 'We could always improvise.'

She bit her lip, half wanting to laugh, half wanting to put him in his place—down, down, down. She decided to change tack. Do the subservient maid thing and see how he felt about that. So she clasped her hands together demurely and let the retort fall back inside. 'Seriously, Blake, what would you like me to do first?'

He looked at her narrowly. 'I wasn't joking about the entertainment.'

'Well…' she gave it some thought '…I'm not so good at dancing, actually, and I've been told my singing is passable but not strong. I can play the piano a little. Do you have a piano?'

He shook his head.

'Well…' she offered a demure smile '…I'm not sure what else to suggest. What do you think?'

'Actually I'm still keen on the belly dancing.' He wasn't smiling. Then he offered his hand. 'Come, let's go out to the deck.'

She looked at the outstretched hand. Slowly put hers in it. As soon as their palms touched his fingers curled, trapping her own. And she knew there was no going back.

He led the way through the large open-plan living area and out the bi-folding doors and she pretended her gasp was over the view, not the currents of electricity surging up her arm. Outside in the blazing sun there was a magnificent deck that flowed down to a large infinity pool, which gave the illusion of the water reaching right out and merging with that of the ocean.

'Wow.' The plants in the pots lining one end of the pool were perfectly maintained, the water crystal-clear, the deck free of debris and clutter. The effect was soothing, relaxing and magical.

'Did you do all this?'

He half snorted. 'I pay.' He looked at it and she could see in his face the pleasure he took from it. 'I oversaw the design.'

'It's beautiful.'

'Thanks.'

She could imagine him swimming length after length; no wonder his body was so tanned, lean and strong. Right now she felt hotter than a cactus in Death Valley in the midday sun and that expanse of water looked incredibly inviting. She turned her back on it to look up at the house.

'You live here alone?'

He nodded.

'It's not too big?'

'I like the peace.' He nodded to the table, with the comfortable-looking chairs around it. A tall pitcher of fresh juice was the centrepiece. They sat, with him angling his chair so he faced her rather than the spectacular pool, and then he poured them each a drink.

She sat bolt upright in her chair, feeling as if she were about to be interviewed for a job she didn't know that she was going to be able to do, but that she really wanted.

Amusement coloured his features. 'Relax, Cally. I'm not going to eat you.' He took a sip from his glass. 'At least, not yet.'

She crossed her legs a little tighter and reached for her own glass. 'I think you'll find there's something else on the menu.'

With a sly smile he set his drink down. 'Tell me about your business.'

'Why?'

His shoulders lifted carelessly. 'It's a big part of your life. I want to understand it better, understand why it's so important to you.'

'OK.' That she could do. She started at the beginning again—her experiments in the kitchen that were motivated by the impudent desire to subvert her mother's diet regimes, then her study in food science and the decision to go into business herself. She didn't go into the decision to have the company donate half its profits to charity—he didn't need to know all that.

But as she talked she relaxed, telling him some of the jokes between her and Mel. The crazy times when they'd worked through the night to prepare enough when the big orders had started rolling in, the crazier times now she had more staff to manage and more customers to satisfy.

'It really is everything to you.'

'It's my baby.' She laughed, hiding the secret stab that came with the knowledge her business ventures were the only babies she'd ever have. 'It keeps me up all night—teething trouble, the works.' She glanced out to where the vivid blue of the pool seemed to meld into the wide blue of the sea. 'Actually, to be honest, it's not so much a baby now as an unruly teenager who I'm thinking of turfing out of the family home.'

'Really?' He laughed.

She nodded, joined in his warm, melodious mirth with a chuckle of her own. 'It's eating up all my resources.'

'Raiding the fridge?'

'And how!' She sighed and her laughter died. 'I think I need a manager. I went into it because I wanted to do the fun bits, you know—the creative stuff, the recipe prep. Let me tell you, management and paperwork is not fun. But the way the business is growing that's what I'm having to do more and more of.'

'But if you gave it up what would you do?'

She grinned. 'I have lots of ideas.'

'I bet you do.'

He nodded and they talked more—business, contracts, supply and demand. Somehow almost an hour passed.

'Are you hungry?'

She was, but not for what he was offering. Why wasn't he offering what she wanted? Had she read this weekend all wrong? Here she'd been thinking they were in for some seriously naughty fun and, while she'd wanted to keep him in his place, she was disappointed that all he was interested in was showing her his house, chatting about work and now feeding her.

'A little.'

As she followed him to his kitchen she realised she was actually a lot hungry. There were some seriously yummy smells wafting in the warm air.

He took oven mitts and lifted a tray out of the oven. She watched, mouth watering as he put the bread on a cooling rack.

'Did you bake this?'

He nodded.

'It's not one of those take-and-bake jobs from the supermarket?'

'Never,' he declared. 'Ever had one of them smell as good as this?'

She poked at it. 'How did you get the crust so…'

'Crusty?' He laughed.

She nodded. 'Not even the French bother baking a French stick in their homes. They go to the baker. You can't get the same crust in a home oven.'

'I don't have a home oven. I have an industrial oven.' She turned and had a good look at the machine fixed into the wall. Industrial was right. You could feed an army cooking with that thing. 'Why? You're some sort of glorified banker, aren't you? Why on earth do you need an oven like this?'

He'd torn some strips of bread and offered her one. 'I like bread. I like baking. I like baking bread.'

'Can you cook anything else?' She munched on the warm loaf.

'Maybe. If I wanted to. I don't want to.'

'Why not have a bread maker?'

He stopped just before taking another bite. 'Why not go to the shop and buy a loaf?'

'But it takes hours. You have to leave it to prove. All that kneading.'

He grinned. 'Exactly. The reward isn't all in the result. The reward is also in the process. Taking the time. Each step along the way. There is nothing like kneading the dough. Rolling it, pushing it, over and over. Then you know it'll rise well, the taste will be superior. It has to be done slowly. It has to be done by hand.'

Her cheeks flushed, trying not to think about the images his words were bringing into her brain. And he knew. She knew he knew. They weren't just talking about bread.

'Like all good things. It takes time.'

'So who taught you to bake bread?' She tried to get a grip. 'Your mother?'

'I taught myself. Mum was at work. I had to eat. The good thing about bread is that you don't need a lot in the way of in-gredients. And the ingredients themselves are cheap. I'd bake bread—big, heavy loaves. And then I'd make toast or sand-wiches. I can make anything into a sandwich.'

Cally processed the info. Understood. He'd been hungry as a kid. 'It was just you and your mother?'

He nodded. 'And you?'

She didn't want to talk personal much any more. Didn't want this to progress beyond anything much more than it was—a dare, a one-weekend-only special. She didn't want to develop feelings for him other than lust, which, hopefully, would soon be sated. It would be all too easy to like him—a lot. Aside from the obvious physical factor, he was interesting, funny. He stood so easy in his own skin. He knew his body and he'd be as comfortable working his way around her body too. He made it all seem so simple.

So she nodded assent and then turned the conversation back. 'You bake often?'

'Fairly. It relaxes me.'

'You don't seem like you'd need relaxing. You seem pretty laid-back. Assured.'

'You think? I get uptight. I certainly get frustrated.' Another innocent smile. 'What do you do to relax, Cally?'

'Same as you. I cook.'

'Aren't we a good combination? I make the bread, you make the soup. Complementary.'

It was too hot in the kitchen. She wanted to get back into the lounge or, even better, the deck. Uptight didn't even begin to describe how she was feeling. She focused on the bread again, studying the thickness of the crust, the texture.

He looked thoughtful. 'You know, the best way to make you understand isn't to tell you, but to show you.'

'Show me what?'

He grinned, as if knowing she wasn't thinking quite along the lines he was. 'How to bake bread.'

Oh. Right. By the time she'd told herself she really wasn't disappointed he'd pulled out a bin of flour from the walk-in pantry.

'You're serious?'

'Absolutely.'

Fascinated she watched as within minutes he had ingredients lined up on the bench and the scales out. A big old-fashioned earthenware bowl sat centre-stage.

'Don't you use an electric mixer?'

'I do everything by hand.' He gestured for her to come beside him. 'Only today, *you* do everything by hand.'

He ran the taps and washed his hands; she followed.

Amused and fascinated she watched; she hadn't baked in years. He measured the flour, took yeast from the fridge, mixed in a little sugar, a little salt, water. Eventually he ditched the wooden spoon to work with his hands and then dumped the dough from the bowl to the bench.

'Now knead.'

He stood aside, and she stepped up to his bench, painfully aware of him behind her, watching over her shoulder. She felt stupid, self-conscious, and with a sigh started pushing at the dough. He watched in silence for a few minutes and she knew he wasn't impressed.

'You need to put your heart into it, Cally,' he chided. 'If you want anything to be any good you have to give it everything. Just let go and get into it.'

Right. With the most gorgeous man ever to walk the planet at her back making her feel as if she were under a microscope. She heard a muffled grouch and then his arms encircled hers, and he put his hands on her own. Slowly he guided her, showing how to work the dough—the way he worked it.

'If you take your time you can feel it growing more pliant.' His voice was almost a whisper.

All she could feel was his length all the way down her back. As she bent forward over the dough it brought her bottom into contact with his groin. She heard his sharp intake of breath and fought the urge to grind back against him, wanting to rotate her hips against his. Instead she pressed back towards the bench, away from him. His hands left hers and he put a fraction more space between them.

She took the frustration out on the dough, rolling it over and over and squishing it and moulding it, pushing her energy into it until it was as smooth and supple and as ready as she already was.

Sweat formed on her forehead and she lost herself in the rhythm of the work.

He didn't move away. She could feel him right there,

watching, but she didn't mind as she lost herself in a kind of sensual trance, the energy flowing from her core to her limbs out from her fingers to the bread.

She didn't know how long she worked. But suddenly his arms came around her again, his hands grasping hers.

'Enough.' His voice rasped in her ear.

She stopped instantly. Realised she was panting. For a long moment they stood, him clasping her. Her heart rate didn't slow, instead it started a less-than-steady increase. 'What now?'

There was a silence before he answered. 'We let it rest. Then do it again.' He let go of her and she sensed him step back.

For a split second she felt relief and then she just felt cold. It took every ounce of inner strength not to turn around and fling herself in his arms like some desperate, clinging female.

Instead she inhaled deeply and turned, trying once more for cool confidence. But then she saw he'd only stepped a little bit away. Now he blocked her path and his eyes were burning. She didn't know what to do or say, but the intense look was slowly killing her.

'Let's go back to the deck,' he muttered, but not moving.

'Are you going to let me past?'

'Maybe. For a price.' The reply dragged from him was so low she had to step closer to hear.

'How much?' She was willing to pay an awful lot.

'A kiss.'

'Just one?' Not brave enough to admit to what she wanted the answer to be.

'For now.'

The intensity didn't lighten at all and there was no smile as he stepped forward. She almost stepped back but his hands went to her shoulders, stopping her flight.

Finally.

Seven long days since they'd touched and it was all she'd been able to think about in that time. At last she was going to get it again—and more. She lifted her face, lips parted, eyelids lowered to half-mast. He slid his hands down her arms, pinning them to her sides, not letting her put them round his neck the way she ached to. Encapsulating her fists in his own, he lowered his head, slowly, staring into her eyes, dropping his attention to lips that she knew would look red—every cell and nerve ending in them was begging for him.

There was no sweet exploration this time. It was straight into plunder territory, with her demanding as much from him.

She felt his grip tighten, felt him take that small step closer. She ached to press right against him. But just as she was about to sway forward he lifted his head with a groan. She blinked, opened her eyes and saw the slight uncertainty in his.

She leaned forward for more, but he gently pushed her back from him. 'Just one, remember?'

He didn't quite meet her eye, didn't smile, just moved her to the side, and stepped forward to the bench. He picked up the ball of dough and placed it back into the bowl, brushed it with oil, covering it carefully with a clean cloth with all the focus and deliberation of a neurosurgeon performing the most complex procedure.

Ridiculously, she felt jealous of the time he took over it. She wanted all that care and attention for herself. He could still think about a loaf of bread after a kiss like that? Something had stopped him. What? And why?

Hell, maybe she could add premature menopause to her list of women's problems. All this hot and cold business was sending her crazy.

CHAPTER SIX

CALLY stood along the edge of the pool and stared longingly at the water.

'Want to swim?'

'I don't have a swimsuit with me.'

'And that's a problem because?' Blake was back, in control and wicked with it. 'It's a very private pool. I don't often bother with shorts myself.'

The flush blanketed her body from tip to toe—as if a hot red sheet had slowly been drawn over her. He watched and the wicked look widened to a smile.

'You sure you don't want to cool down?'

She turned, anger flaring. 'You're the one who needs to cool down.' She pushed, totally catching him by surprise, and he tumbled straight in.

The satisfaction at seeing the splash was sublime. The giggles burst out. She delighted at seeing him toppled for once, watching as he stretched out under the water, turning around and heading back to the edge at which she stood.

She made sure she stepped back just far enough out of arm's reach. She underestimated. In a move that totally surprised her he leapt from the water. Easily hooking his arm around her knees and heaving her over his shoulder so she went head first into the pool. It was not a graceful entry—her arms and legs were in all directions and she knew the splash was spectacular. She sank deep and took her time about coming up. When she surfaced he was standing, chest-deep and looking fiery.

'You deserve a dunking for that, my sweet,' he warned, peeling his tee shirt off his head.

The feeling of delight multiplied. 'You'll have to catch me first.' With a laugh she dived away, quite happy for him to play catch.

Her jeans were heavy, weighing her down and clinging uncomfortably to her legs, but she didn't care. His hand encircled her arm, he pulled her to her feet and within close range. Water racing down her face, she shivered, cold from the pool, hot for him.

He stared into her face, as if he was searching for an answer to a question she didn't know had been asked.

'Take your jeans off and swim in your undies. I'm going to do a few lengths.' He let her go again and dived in the other direction. Mystified, she watched him escape. He was deliberately keeping his distance.

She stood up in the shallow end and dragged off her shirt. Sodden, it landed with a squelchy thud on the concrete surround. Her jeans were trickier to remove and in the end she had to float on her back as she wriggled them down. She stood on the step to throw them out of the pool, enjoying the warm beat of the sun on her wet skin. As she turned back to the water she saw he'd stopped swimming, was just treading water in the deep end and staring.

She glanced down and discovered neither her bra nor her undies remained opaque when wet—no. Both were utterly transparent.

And he was looking at her as if he'd never seen a near naked woman before.

The flush returned to her body. All the blood rushed to the surface and she felt hotter than the sun.

His answering flush was something else. She hadn't known it was possible for a tanned man to flush like that. But the colour slashed across high cheekbones and his sea-green eyes were lit by a matching flame.

'I thought the water was supposed to cool us off,' she croaked.

'Must be some sort of chemical thing.' He coughed. 'If you go into the pool house you'll find towels and spare bathrobes hanging. And toiletries and stuff. Have a shower or whatever and put on a robe while your clothes dry. I'm going to do another length.'

He turned and splashed through the water again.

Uncaring about the drips, she padded through the pool house—a perfectly good home in itself. Why he lived in such a mansion all by himself puzzled her, but what puzzled her more was why he kept holding back when it was plain as day that they were both pretty eager to get close. That the effect they had on each other was undeniable. What was he waiting for?

She glanced at her watch—glad it was water resistant. She'd been here for hours and other than that one shattering kiss in the kitchen he'd made no move. What had happened to his promise of six big Os in the one night? She wanted that, damn it. Hell, even just one. OK, two. She'd be happy enough with that.

When was he going to get on with it because she didn't know if she could wait any longer. And then it hit her—why should she wait? Maybe she should be honest, it was why she was here after all. Couldn't she initiate? Maybe she could be the one not taking no for an answer.

The thrill rippled through her entire body. She stood for a moment under the powerful shower and mentally deliberated. Forcing the recollections of her time with Luc from her mind—they always snuck in at times when she wanted to be brave.

Take what you want, Cally. Take what you want.

She lathered the creamy gel on her body, breathing in the fresh floral fragrance, smoothing it into her skin and starting to feel like a siren preparing herself for seduction.

By the time she left the pool house he was out of the water. Presumably he was in the main building. She spread her sodden clothes on the wooden deckchairs to dry and then turned—it was time.

Blake stood in his kitchen and watched as she walked towards him. He was nearly at breaking-point and seeing her like this was pretty much the last straw. She'd knotted the robe firmly at the waist. She had no make-up on. Her hair was slick. She was beautiful and utterly ready for bed.

He'd been holding back all day. Biding his time, waiting for the right moment. Because he didn't just want her willing, he wanted her wild. He wanted to know she was as out of control for him as he was for her.

That moment in the kitchen had been a mistake, but one he hadn't been able to resist. He'd had to pull back quickly from a kiss that had threatened to send every rational thought out the window for all eternity. And that had thrown him. That she seemed to be able to make him forget anything and everything just by touching him.

He'd had to prove to himself that he could pull back. Transient lust. That was all this was, and soon to be remedied because, hell, it was crippling.

He looked back to the kitchen bench and reminded himself of his plan. He didn't just want victory. He wanted total surrender.

'You were so long in the shower I did round two of the bread and put it in the oven.' He couldn't have coped to see her hands on that dough again. He opened the fridge. 'Wine?'

'Thank you.' She accepted the glass he held out and with deliberation lifted it straight to her lips and took a long, deep sip, not breaking eye contact with him the entire time. Then she lowered the glass, set it on the bench next to her and came closer to him—intention apparent in every move.

His pulse picked up. 'Got something you want to say, Cally?'

'No.'

He knew now. She was ready. And, please God, let him be able to handle it. She stepped closer. He looked down at her plump lips, deep pink and parted.

She was his. But he refused to leave room for regret. And he had a lesson for her—one he didn't want her to forget in a hurry. He whispered, mouth millimetres from hers. An almost kiss.

'There's something I want you to do for me.'

Her eyes were cloudy, acquiescent, desire-drugged.

He walked to the kitchen drawers and pulled out the length of black fabric from the second one down, where he'd stashed it earlier. He held it out and it unfolded into a mask.

She looked at him wide-eyed.

He smiled. 'Nothing kinky, honey. But I do have a test for you.' He spoke quickly, not wanting the heat in her face to be replaced by fear or uncertainty. 'You say you have bad taste, that you have terrible judgment. I think you're wrong. So what if you made a mistake in the past? I think you need to trust your instincts more. So I have a selection here—of fake and of genuine. Fake maple syrup and the real thing, pure virgin olive oil and the chemical crap they mislabel, genuine French champagne and synthetic bubbles. See where I'm going with this?'

'This is like some game at a kid's party.'

'Right. The blind taste test. Maybe your judgment will be better when you can't see. Interesting idea, don't you think?'

Her lips twitched and he relaxed, pulling out one of the kitchen stools, which she immediately hopped on. He set out the items on the bench in front of her. A small smile played on her mouth—she was buying in now, well and truly.

'Close your eyes.' This time he didn't need to tell her twice. Her lids fluttered shut and he suppressed the flare of satisfaction at the sight of her quick and quiet acquiescence. He placed the silk band over her eyes and tied it at the back. Without her eyes on him he was able to study her freely.

The need for her was intense and the need to know she wanted him as badly was even more intense.

'Let's start with the champagne.'

Her breathing had accelerated, just a fraction, but he was so attuned to her he picked it up right away. Faster and shorter. He poured a small amount from each bottle into two glasses, then held them in turn to her lips, watching as she drank.

'Which is it, the first or the second?' He set the glasses down as she deliberated.

'The first.'

'Right first time.'

The smile on her lips deepened.

'Now the oil. I'll dip a little bread in some, OK?'

He stood close, fascinated, as her mouth took each morsel in, her tongue appearing out for a tantalising time to lick the crumb from her lips.

'The second.'

'Correct,' he muttered.

'And now the syrup.' He poured some straight from the bottle onto his index finger and held it up to her lips. Stroked their softness just a little, to tease her. 'Suck it off.'

He waited, tormented, as the colour tinged her cheeks. And then her mouth opened and she took him in. Her tongue swirled around his finger and then she gripped and he nearly groaned, the gentle tugging of her mouth an erotic experience unlike any other. He didn't want to pull out. But he did, replacing it with the other finger, the other syrup, and he no longer cared about anything but how soon he could get the rest of him into her like this. Hot and wet and just how he wanted her.

'Which is it?' he whispered hoarsely.

She shook her head a little. 'I'm not sure. I think I need to try them again.'

Minx.

He did groan then, half delight, half amusement, wholly desire. 'I think we should skip it and move on.'

'There's more?'

'A lot more.' He paused, only a second longer. 'What about this, Cally? Is this genuine?'

And he pressed his mouth to hers, tasted the last of the sweet, sticky syrup. And then it was just her and she tasted divine.

'Does this feel real to you, Cally?'

'It feels…it feels…'

'This is real. Full-on roaring lust, Cally. You want me and I want you.' As he'd never wanted another—so intensely it stirred him almost to anger. *She* made him angry—constantly forcing him to reassess, constantly making him feel the need to defend himself. He didn't want her on a whim, because of some bet. He simply had no choice. From the moment he'd seen her he'd sensed the depths, felt the primal recognition of the perfect—physical—mate.

He wanted it to be the same for her. Wanted her to feel this almost animal need to have, to dominate, to possess. To surrender.

It smelt real; it tasted real; it felt real.

She couldn't think any more. As his hands held her head, and his tongue swept into her mouth to taste all of her, she felt it through to her marrow. The very real lust. The need to have him keep kissing her like this—long and deep and so, so sweet and hot.

He whispered into her ear, his breath warm and tickling, and all she wanted was that mouth back on hers.

'I'm not going to do anything that you aren't willing for me to do. You can say no and I'll stop. OK?'

As if she was going to say no.

'There's just me and there's just you and we're just going to have some fun.'

Bring it on.

'This is what you want, right?'

He still needed to ask? Couldn't he feel the way she was trembling? Couldn't he feel the fire that burned through her veins? 'Yes.' She wanted him to stop thinking, stop questioning, stop talking. She just wanted him to take her. She knew he could make her go places she'd never been, had only dreamed being. He could do that with just one kiss. Now she wanted the rest of it.

He spun her on the stool so the bench was at her back. She heard him walk and then felt him in front of her, felt his fingers in her hair, and could hardly wait.

But as the mask slipped from her skin, so the blinding lust cooled and a speck of reason peeked in. She looked at him. Really looked at him, looking at her. And she couldn't believe what was in his eyes.

He pushed the robe from her shoulders, so it slid down her arms, and started to slip from her body. Half naked, she looked down and felt uncomfortable.

This man was perfection. She was not.

'I think I preferred it with the blindfold on.'

His brows lifted. 'So you can't see me?'

'So I can't see *me*.'

'You think you're ugly?'

'No. But I'm not a model.' It wasn't that she was ugly. She was ordinary. Ordinarily ordinary wouldn't matter. But when you were the daughter of a supermodel? Then it was a problem. She was miles off that striking, classical bone structure—the perfect, symmetrical face. And as for her figure. 'I'm not slim.'

'No.' He grinned. 'But who wants a bag of bones?' He rested his hands on her shoulders, thumbs stroking, soothing her smooth skin.

'Let me tell you what I see.' He looked, a long, measuring look down her body, and she would have scrambled for some sort of covering if his hands weren't firm on her arms, holding her still for his inspection. 'I look at your breasts. I look at your belly. I look at your heaven-sent bottom and my brain shuts down. Instinct screams at me—fecundity! Fertile female. Must procreate, must procreate.' A sharp smile, a mocking edge and an even keener look in his eye.

She stared at him. And finally, she laughed. A short brittle crack.

'Which shows how appearances can be deceiving, I guess. You males can't do intuition or instinct.' She stood up, clutching the robe, walked away from the kitchen and into the living area. 'I'm never having children.'

The silence was small but pointed. 'You're a career woman through and through?' He followed her, stood beside her, heat radiating from him. She knew it wasn't just lust spiking his temperature—there was anger too.

Let him judge. He knew nothing of her heartbreak, the way her body's limitations had forced her to take a road she'd rather be off but that she was determined to make the best of.

'Absolutely. Nothing matters more to me than my business.' Bitterness made her vehement, and self-hatred sounded simply like hate.

His eyes flashed fire. Did he think she was some heartless, hard-headed workaholic lacking any kind of maternal instinct? She wasn't—but so what if she was? It wasn't by choice. He could think what he liked—she was determined not to care.

They stared at each other, passion clashing. But the blast of temptation and desire was too strong, transforming her emotion from angry disappointment to angry lust. Despite his obvious disapproval, despite the fact he was exactly the wrong type for her, she still wanted him. She saw the same battle in his eyes and knew that neither of them wanted to feel things this way—forced beyond boundaries that normally were easy to maintain.

'Just us.' She stated the rules. 'Just sex.' She looked at his expression. There was no smile. No tenderness. It was purely dark desire that would disappear once they'd done it. 'Right?'

'Right.'

He stepped towards her, ripped his fresh tee shirt over his

head, shrugged out of the jeans and was gloriously naked in less than two seconds.

Her mouth, like her robe, fell to the floor. She no longer cared about her body, she only cared about his—about getting her hands on the utterly perfect form before her.

They stepped forward, any polite hesitation abandoned. It had already taken too long. His mouth fastened onto hers, tongue searching. Leaving no doubt as to what he wanted, what he was going to have. And from the speed with which they were both moving, he was going to have it all soon.

The last of her anger was consumed in flames of desire as his big hands weighed her breasts; her tight nipples begged to be taken into his hot mouth but it was his thumbs that teased them. She shifted restlessly, rocking her hips towards him. He bent his head to kiss down her neck and suddenly her legs couldn't seem to hold her weight any more. He caught her against him and took them down to the floor together.

They kissed and touched like the sensation-starved. She *was* starved, and she badly wanted everything she sensed he could give her—that release, that completion.

His fingers sought her out, curving into her. He lifted his head and his eyes glowed. 'You're wet for me.'

She nodded, boldly reaching out to him. 'You're hard for me.'

He grinned, tight, his anger forgotten too as anticipation sharpened. 'Definitely some sort of reaction.'

And then he made her wetter, with his fingers teasing, swirling, stroking at the particularly sensitive area just north of where she wanted to bury the hot, hard length she had in her hand now. She squeezed him firmer and his fingers worked faster. She stretched her legs as wide and as tight as she could, driving her hips back and forth towards him and her hand hard up and down him. She wanted to master him, wanted to make him take her—completely. His breathing was choppy, as was hers, and, groaning, he grabbed her hand with a death grip, stopping her from rubbing him, yet continuing to torment her with his other extremely clever hand.

And then he slid down her body, replacing those fingers with his mouth, and all she could do was lie there and let him nuzzle into her, so intimate and so intense. He kissed and licked and then the fingers were back too, sliding right inside while his scalding mouth sucked deep.

Sensations were rushing on her now—but she didn't want to burst yet, not like this.

'No!' she called desperately. 'No, no, no. It's cheating.'

He froze, moved to look into her face. His grip bruising her wrist. 'Cally? *Cheating?*'

She curved into him, pressing her hips against his as she realised he thought she meant something else entirely. If she was going to get what she wanted she'd better spell it out for him. This was a one-weekend-only special. She had nothing to lose and the chance for an experience of a lifetime. Why let nerves or embarrassment ruin that now? So, despite knowing her cheeks must be purple, she spoke. 'I want to come when you're...when we're...'

The black thunder cloud lifted from his brow. 'You want me inside you when you come?'

She nodded. 'I want you to come too.'

There was a grunt of laughter. 'That's not going to be a problem, sweetheart.'

'Six for six.'

'No problem.' His hands moved to caress her breasts, teasing her nipples. 'We'll do it your way this first time, but I want to taste you as you come one time, though.'

Heat flamed her cheeks further. 'Ditto.'

His fingers flicked faster. 'Definitely not a problem.'

They kissed again then, finally on the same page. His hips settled between hers and she felt the silken head of him pressing at her wet entrance.

He surged forward, one long stroke, filling her completely—hard.

Her head fell back, throat bared to him in ultimate sur-render, and her eyes fluttered, the cry coming from some primal place deep within as she felt every glorious inch of him push deep.

He stilled. And then slowly he pulled back, almost leaving her body completely. She opened her eyes at that and was about to complain when he surged forward again, even harder. The completion, the satisfaction at finally having him there, made her cry out again, raw.

In a tormentingly slow rhythm he retreated again. She moaned, wanting him to move faster. Her hands slid harshly up his upper arms, she spread her fingers on the broad bunch of his shoulder, the tips curling into the muscle, pressing deep on the bone. She cried out again as he hit her with another powerful thrust.

Her breath hissed as he tipped back once more. She saw the confident smile on his face had been wiped and was replaced by concentration on her and wholly on her. 'Cally,' he muttered.

Her legs locked, muscles burning with tightness, and she dug her heels into the carpet, pushing her hips up to meet his with all her strength.

And this time, as he thrust to meet her it wasn't a cry. It was a scream.

Shudders ravaged through her; wave upon wave of almost unbearable ecstasy washed over her from head to toe. Her body contracted around him, again and again, squeezing out the satisfaction it had too long been denied.

She heard his choke, felt him pumping hard and fast, his breathing harsh in a crazy rhythm. And suddenly a groan—relief mixed with disbelief.

As her own breathing started to settle, she happily, languor-ously, took his weight. His big body sprawled over hers, she ran her hands idly down his back, loving the breadth of the muscles under her fingers and the slick heat pouring off him.

He lifted his head and the look on his face was definitely rueful. 'Well, that happened a little sooner than I expected.'

'Are you kidding? I've been here *all* day.'

Laughter shook his chest.

'Oh, you mean—'

'Yeah.' He kept his hips pressed to hers, so they were still joined. The colour in his cheeks deepened. 'You've got a bit of a punch.'

'Chemical reaction, I guess.' She grinned, unable to hide the pleasure she got at the realisation he hadn't held onto his control the way he'd wanted. She arched up to him a little, stretching out the tension in her body that was already coiling again.

He grinned. 'Definitely one major explosion.' He bent his head to her breast, blew warm air on the nipple that strained up to him. 'One down, five to go. I think we need the follow-up soon. That was over all too quick.'

This time, it wasn't over quick at all. He carried her to his bedroom, in swashbuckling pirate style, and set about driving her crazy in slow, torturous fashion.

They dozed for a while, she lay half awake, half asleep— her body so wired she wondered if she'd ever truly sleep again.

He rolled away, pulled her to her feet and, keeping hold of her hand, led her to a big bathroom most definitely designed for two. They stood under the shower, just kissing, and he ran his soapy hands down her back. Holding her close, not demanding more, but just long soothing kisses until she was the one moving restlessly, the one driving for more—and drive she did with kisses and caresses that became increasingly insistent, confidence growing as she saw the degree to which she could arouse him. She let her fingers glide over his muscles, the wet bronzed wall that was his chest, then stepped out of the reach of the water, turned and knelt before him.

His eyes were large and flaming as he looked down at where she waited with hands and mouth ready. 'Are you sure?'

'You've proven to me what good taste I have. Let me taste this.'

He groaned and she started playing, tracing fingers over his body, moving in circles ever closer to his magnificent erection—kissing, stroking, touching, teasing.

His thighs were rigid and his hands ran through her hair, mussing it as she pressed her mouth to him.

'Cally…' She heard the mutter and felt passion stirring in him, the barely leashed movement in his hips. He was close. She gripped firmer, faster—signalling her intention to see him through, to take it, taste it all. Another heartfelt groan escaped him, pelvis pistoning, fingers twisting in her hair as he gave in, gave her control, gave her everything.

She revelled in his hoarse cry, in feeling his powerful body racked with pleasure, in the extreme explosion she'd asked for.

And when she'd taken what she wanted, he reached out a hand and pulled her to her feet. He leaned sideways against the wall, his back still taking the water of the shower, breathing deep, clearly recovering.

He looked at her with slightly rueful eyes. 'Taste good?'

She nodded, drunk on desire, on the thrill of seeing him so tortured, knowing she'd done that.

He shook his head. 'I'll give you something that tastes even better.' He picked her up and carried her through to his bed, spreading her body to his satisfaction and starting an exploration that was so slow, so intense, so erotically charged she honestly thought she'd die from the pleasure. His hands and mouth roved the length of her, worshipping, arousing. Eventually he centred on the centre of her—sucking, licking, his tongue going deep, seeking out her essence, the proof of her attraction. Unbearable heat flooded her and she tossed her head, clenching her teeth to stop the screams.

His hands reached up and found her breasts, fingers working on her nipples, toying with their hardness as his tongue worked faster and faster. She couldn't stop her hips from rocking up to him, couldn't contain the shattering climax. And as the final shudders were still rippling through her he rose and lay over her. Kissing her deeply, he let her taste herself and him together—such profound and naked intimacy she'd never before experienced. It just turned her on even more.

She felt the hard length of him against her thigh and looked at him—surprised to feel his renewed desire and deep inside her own sizzling again. 'I thought I'd drained you. Your stamina is incredible.'

'Only because you're so insatiable.' He paused above her, face and body rigid as he stated it plainly. 'Aren't you? Hungry for me.'

'Yes.' She whispered the unnecessary answer, tilting her hips up to him. She could never get enough. And he pushed inside once more—his tongue, his penis. He totally invaded, claiming her, and she welcomed his possession, arching up, opening up, wanting more and more. Deeper, harder, faster, longer.

For a few hours they slept, curled together, arms and legs entwined. Once she was awake, her fourth and fifth orgasms came in rapid succession—in the one session. She didn't want to admit to both of them. She wanted to sneak in another round. Multiples counted as one, really, didn't they? She smiled as she drifted back to sleep, she'd never have thought she'd get to one, let alone go multiple.

As soon as she woke again she turned towards him.

'You owe me more. You promised. Worried you can't make it?'

'You sure you're keeping the right score?' He grinned, eyes twinkling with good humour and a lusty light. He knew all right. But he wasn't arguing.

This time, the feeling of goodness radiated out through her body. Till she felt it was powerful enough to be an entity in its own right. Magic swirled around their entwined bodies, encapsulating them, imprisoning them, while still being part of them.

She welcomed the slickness between her thighs. The smell,

the sweat, the slipperiness that came with sex. Sex as she'd never had before. And knew she'd never have again—unless it was with him.

He only gave her another couple of hours to recover before starting a massage that ended with her writhing. Then he led her back to the shower where he took her from behind before spinning her round and starting all over again, driving her crazy, making her come, until the water finally ran cold.

CHAPTER SEVEN

WITH every step Cally's whole body throbbed, so sensitive, so well used in the last twenty-four hours that she knew she couldn't take any more—not physically. Certainly not emotionally. She tiptoed to the bathroom, leaving Blake sleeping soundly in the big bed, only partly covered by the white cotton sheet. She wasn't going to look at him to be tempted either—much.

She was utterly exhausted. Everything seemed to be tilted topsy-turvy and she had to get away—now, or she never would. At least not still in one piece.

She splashed cold water on her face and assessed the situation. She had to concede she was in the presence of a master. Yesterday he'd started it slow, kept it almost like a date, getting her to relax by talking about her business. Then he'd got her warmed up—progressively warmer until she'd been the one to blow on the crackling embers to burst them into flame.

All they'd done since was have sex and then sleep together. Have sex some more and then sleep. Repeat again. Conversation had been minimal. Only sharing the words needed to convey pleasure and desire, need and want.

In the light of day awkwardness had barrelled into the room and was holding her up. Words now were required. And they'd build the barriers she so desperately needed. Because she was vulnerable and raw and weakly just wanted to return to the haven that was his embrace. But it was a false haven. This was meaningless for him—he'd said it from the start: just some fun with no future, no trust necessary. She didn't like him for that.

But she'd said it too. Just sex?

All too late she realised she couldn't play that kind of game. So, tempting as it was not to, she had to finish with him here and now.

He was sitting up in bed when she stepped back out of the bathroom. She was glad to see his perfect features bore signs of their night. His jaw was darkened by stubble, his eyes also shadowed—by fatigue.

She attempted breeziness. 'I need to get going.'

He said nothing, just watched her with eyes that burned.

'I have to…um…'

He slid from the bed and pulled on jeans—didn't bother with undies or tee shirt. She lost her train of thought.

'You want some breakfast?' He fastened the buttons on his fly.

Had he even heard her?

'Before you head home?'

He'd heard her all right. And he wasn't about to argue.

'I'll just get my things.'

She walked out the doors—still open—to the deck by the pool. She tugged on her crumpled jeans—not bothering with the scrappy knickers or the bra hanging on the arm of the chair. She yanked on the tee, stuffed the underwear into her back pocket and hoped she wouldn't see anyone on the street.

She turned. He was standing across the deck, leaning against the doorway with a mug in his hands, watching her every move. He sipped from the steaming liquid.

She looked around for her shoes and found them under the table.

'You don't even want a coffee?'

What was with his host-with-the-most act? Couldn't he see she was desperate to escape? Before she showed how desperately she wanted back in his arms. Desperately begging for more than he could give—would ever want to give. She had pride to maintain here.

Blake had no idea how to settle her. But he didn't want her to go yet. And he vainly searched for ways to make her stay a little longer.

'What about brunch?' It was way past breakfast and frankly he could do with some food. He was getting light-headed. 'I'm good with eggs.'

He saw her nose wrinkle in distaste. 'No, thanks. I really do need to get going. I've got some work I need to do.'

He watched as she looked anywhere but at him. Back to that again—denial.

'Cally—'

'Thanks for everything.' She flashed the brittle smile he hated. He had another sip of coffee and let the black, lethally strong liquid fire down to his belly. Hopefully it would get his brain working. Because right now he had serious Neanderthal Man urges to overcome.

'Cally, I think we need to talk.' He'd rather they didn't; he'd rather they just go back to his bed. Contact, physical contact, would sort everything if they had enough of it. And they hadn't had enough of it yet.

The brittle smile became even more brittle. 'Let's not, Blake.'

'Why not?' Hell, what woman didn't want to talk?

'There's nothing to say, is there? This was a deal. You won. I paid. Now we're done.'

He blinked. She was referring to that stupid bet? If this was a game, he was fast forgetting the rules.

'Our business is finished.'

'You think?'

'You know it is.'

Blake knew nothing of the sort. All he knew was that his

perfect weekend was coming to a close and he didn't want it to. He wanted a repeat—next weekend, please. No, that was too far away. Maybe Wednesday. Or Tuesday. Or, hell, why not tomorrow? But she'd gone all finishing school on him. Back to the frigidly polite woman who determinedly avoided his eyes so he couldn't see the fire they both knew was still there.

She turned quickly and headed to the door.

He hastened after her. 'I'll walk you to your car.'

'That's not nec—'

'Cally.'

She stopped her verbal protest but her body still oozed battle.

With every step towards her car he felt the energy in his body return. Tension rising until he was as pent up as he'd been all week. So much for one night being enough to get rid of it. She pressed the button on her keyring so the car beeped and its lights flashed. It was unlocked, but she'd gone as impenetrable as the Rock of Gibraltar. The need to conquer flared through him.

She reached for the handle, but he reached for her first. His eyes narrowed as he took in her frozen expression. He liked his chocolate warm and melting, not cold and hard.

He sandwiched her between the car and his body. He slid his hand around her neck and worked his fingers into the silky mass that was her hair. It looked so perfect yet felt so soft. He curled strands round his fingers and tugged, so she tilted her head up to his. Then he kissed her.

He kissed her and kissed her. Long and deep, until he felt her arms around him, felt her holding on tight and stroking him, pulling him closer. A final dig of his hips into hers gave him the moan from her that he'd been seeking—total surrender.

With strength he'd never known he had he lifted his hands from her, pressed them onto the car and levered his body off hers. Every cell in his body protested and he clamped down on all his muscles, stopping them from moving the way they so desperately wanted to—back into her. Leaning a millimetre away, he stared moodily into her face. Her lips were red and plump, the shadows under her eyes were pronounced and she wouldn't look back at him. Hiding away. *Running* away.

OK, so they both needed some time and distance. But this wasn't over. He wasn't sure what it was, but it wasn't over.

'See you 'round.'

As a parting shot it was weak but it was the best he could come up with given his conflicting feelings—let alone those so obviously fighting within her. They'd take a day or so to regroup, reassess and then return to the table. Because this deal most definitely wasn't done.

Cally drove the long way home. She should probably hate herself. Hadn't she just done what she'd always vowed she'd never do? *Paid* for a guy? OK, it had been a bet that he'd won but it was still nothing more than a 'transaction', a coldly planned encounter that meant nothing. For whatever reason he'd wanted her and so they'd struck their bargain. There was nothing more on offer from or for either of them.

It had been heaven. Pure heaven.

Only now she felt lonelier than ever.

If she closed her eyes she could still feel him—feel the way he liked to twist and tangle his fingers in her hair. She could still taste him. Most definitely still smell him. She couldn't shake him from her head at all. And she couldn't help but want more. Lots more.

Cally had a soft heart. She worked hard to keep it protected because soft hearts bruised really easily and she didn't like how much that could hurt. Her heart was already half in his hands and she knew how strong his hands were. He wouldn't just bruise her heart, he'd crush it completely. So she had to claim it back and the only way she could do that was to remove herself from temptation.

One of the good things about being wealthy was the fact she

had more than one residence. She had the apartment she used mostly when in town and she had the big sprawling manor with too many childhood memories for her to be able to use and which she rented out as much as she could. And she had the bolt-hole on the vineyard deep in the New South Wales wine country from where she could manage her business remotely when she needed country air and escape. Definitely time to take a trip—because when she went back to Sydney she wanted to have forgotten.

She spent a couple of weeks reacquainting herself with the local town and the surrounding countryside. It should have worked a treat in terms of distraction—except that every time she so much as looked at her car, let alone drove in it, she was reminded of him. She'd sell it as soon as she got back to the city.

She attributed the tiredness to lack of sleep. She worked later and later, hoping to exhaust herself to the point where she'd just collapse in bed and sleep dreamlessly. But as soon as her body hit the sheets she was wide awake and wanting to be back in his bed, not her cold, lonely one. When she finally did sleep it was only to dream—fiery dreams starring Blake and nothing but Blake, buck naked.

Memories tormented her day and night. She could still feel his body covering hers, the brush of hair on his thigh against hers, his arms tight around her waist, the fit of their bodies as they snuggled close to sleep after. All she wanted was him inside her, filling her, giving her that release. My God, she'd never realised that sex could be so addictive, so all-consuming.

Days passed and sleepless nights dragged and she started to feel like a walking wreck. The country escape had failed for the first time and she headed back to town and to work. Only once there the tiredness left her prone to illness.

'Cally, are you OK?' Mel called through the bathroom door.

'Tummy bug.'

'You shouldn't be here. You can't go poisoning all the customers—Health and Safety will shut us down and I'll lose my job.'

'What would it matter?' Right now Cally felt so dreadful she couldn't care less. 'Your fiancé is loaded.'

'It's important to my sense of security to be financially independent. As your employee I'm ordering you to go home.'

Cally half staggered out the bathroom door and leaned on her table.

Mel looked cheeky and concerned at the same time. 'See you.'

'Tomorrow.'

For over a fortnight Blake tried to forget her. And failed. Finally, halfway into the third week, with his body screaming its tension to him, he accepted the fact that he was going to chase and chase hard. There'd been no contact between them since she'd left in such a hurry that Sunday morning. Regrets perhaps? He couldn't see how anyone could regret sex that good. The only thing to regret was that they hadn't had more.

She intrigued him—hadn't been anything like he'd imagined she would. After the auction he'd anticipated some hardened, spoilt society heiress who'd never done a day's real work in her life, a brat playing at being a businesswoman. But, boy, he'd been wrong. She had a brain, talent, ambition. She was able to admit to her weaknesses, able to laugh. Easy to talk to. Easy to tease.

And when he'd touched her? When she'd touched him?

Her generosity, her genuine response had floored him, fired him—no way was he not having that again.

Only this time he wanted to be better prepared and to have a plan for the future. When considering any kind of business transaction Blake was meticulous about due diligence—he'd get his info together beforehand and work out his acquisition or merger strategy from there. Cally Sinclair was no different from any other company target, she was just a personal target; that was all.

She'd declared her intention not to have a family, a fact which still, irrationally, angered him. This anger was especially stupid considering he had no intention of having a family himself. But anger aside it meant, on the face of it, they'd be a good match for a very adult arrangement—one of mutual pleasure and minimal risk. Now he just had to put the package together in such a way that she'd be unable to resist buying in. And to do that, he needed more knowledge.

He buzzed Judith into his office. She ambled in. Hell, could her belly get any bigger?

'Sit.' He pointed to the chair irritably. 'How much longer are you here?'

'Just over a month.'

He frowned. 'Shouldn't you be decorating the nursery or something?'

'Or something,' she agreed affably. 'What can I do for you?'

Blake gave up. 'I want to know everything about Cally's Cuisine.'

'The soup company?'

'That's the one.'

'Cally Sinclair runs it, doesn't she?' Her brain was quick as lightning. 'Didn't she buy you at the auction?' She didn't even try to hide her obscene level of interest.

'Yeah.' He watched Judith's cunning look grow. He sighed. He didn't want to know what she was thinking. But he needed to know more about Cally. And if anyone could find out the gossip about someone, Judith could.

'When you say you want to know everything…?'

'I mean, *everything*.'

Judith's smile was wicked now. She rose. 'Your wish…'

He grunted and told her to shut the door behind her. Then called through the wood. 'As fast as possible.'

Cally leaned against the refrigerator and sighed. This tiredness was not going away, nor was the sickness. The vomiting had ceased but she still felt queasy. Mel looked at her again and Cally tried to mask the feeling she knew was all over her face.

'Are you sure you're well enough to be in here?'

'I'm sure. You go get your things. I'll be fine.'

The lunch rush was over—that time from eleven to two when Mel was run off her feet serving customers fresh, hot soup. The quiet spell came between two and three—and then picked up again as people slipped in to get a container to take home for dinner. So this was when Mel took her break and Cally took to the shop floor—if she hadn't already. She could have one of the kitchen staff do it, but she liked keeping an eye on the customers. Seeing firsthand which soups were most popular. Talking to the customers about what they liked, what they didn't.

Thankfully today the quiet hour was really quiet and after a few late-lunching customers Cally was able to sit on the stool behind the counter and listlessly flick through the latest addition to Mel's pile of bridal mags. Over two thousand pages of powder-puff or meringuey dresses to choke over.

She couldn't seem to stop thinking about Blake. She was getting so bad she'd decided to make a soup in his honour. Something with even more texture and bite—because he certainly had both—and one taste would never be enough. It would be so divine the customers would be beating down the door to get more. If only she could distil and bottle the essence of him she'd be a billionaire businesswoman and not merely a millionaire heiress.

She really needed to stop thinking about him, because she was not going to beat down *his* door. Not going to be another statistic along his highway of conquests. She'd taken her leave early and wasn't going back. But, hell, she couldn't stop the fantasies.

She channelled the desire and debated the bite—chilli, definitely chilli, in a big, thick soup to satisfy the hungriest of appetites. She knew what it was to be hungry and she knew how well he could fill her.

She glanced again at the clock and saw with relief the hands had finally moved and Mel should be back any moment so she could slither to her office, or maybe home. This damn bug was taking for ever to work its way out of her system. Lovesick, she mocked bitterly, that was what she was—or *lust*-sick.

The door opened and Cally dragged herself to her feet, not wanting to look such a layabout in front of a customer.

The blonde was pretty and as pregnant as it was possible to be. She looked puffy in the face and hot and Cally was amazed she wanted soup at all. She looked at the fridge and gave Cally a conspiratorial grin.

'Do you have any cold soups?'

'Like gazpacho?'

As Cally moved the nausea rose and the walls started wobbling. Oh, hell, she wasn't going to faint again, was she?

'Are you OK?' Curious concern was clear in her customer's gaze and Cally lowered hers to avoid it. She stared at the round belly. A sudden suspicion gripped her. She felt warmth flooding into her cheeks. She managed to ask.

'When are you due?'

'Just over a month.'

And the thoughts swirling in her head were so dizzying, so impossible and yet so true. She couldn't believe it. Could hardly dare to think it. Excitement and hope and incredulity flooded her and in the craziness her brain decided it couldn't cope—it needed to descend into darkness to meditate on the idea a while.

She came round and stared into Mel's concerned face.

'Cally, not again!' Mel was on her knees beside her, clutching at Cally's upper arms, rubbing them as if she were cold.

Cally threw her a 'settle down' look.

Mel wasn't having it. 'You have to go home. See a doctor. This has gone on too long to be some bug.'

Cally looked over to see if the customer had left. No. The pregnant woman was looking right back at her. For a suspended moment their gazes met and meshed. Recognition flowed between the two. A shared knowledge.

Cally grinned, the first huge, natural beam in three weeks. Unstoppable delight. And the curious question in the customer's eye settled into certainty.

'Mel, I'm fine. Really. I'm absolutely fine. In fact, I'm fantastic.'

'I've got that info you wanted.'

It was first thing the day after he'd asked her. Judith could always be relied upon to deliver the goods. He'd hired her immediately on application. She had drive, dedication and was completely and utterly competent. And she was thoroughly in love with her husband, which meant there wasn't any risk of unwanted attraction or distraction. He wasn't looking forward to having to replace her. She also had a social networking system like no one else he'd ever encountered. Which was why she'd been the one to hit up unsuspecting males for the bachelor auction.

Today he could see she looked agitated. Usually her eyes sparkled and good humour shone from her—even when he was being demanding. But now she looked troubled and, yes, apprehensive. He sat very still and braced himself. Whatever it was, she didn't want to tell him and that gave him the feeling he didn't want to hear it.

'Tell all.'

'You know the state of the business already—you can see from the sales sheet there. I've pulled the most recent mentions in the paper—social stories as well as business. Seems she's pretty active in the charity scene although not obviously so. No significant male interest. In fact you could say she's conspicuously single. She's known as a workaholic.'

'What else?' He gripped the pencil that little bit tighter. 'Spit it out, Judith.'

His secretary sighed and looked him straight in the eye. 'I think she might be pregnant.'

'What?'

'I think she's pregnant.'

Blake picked up the two pieces of the pencil and tossed them into the rubbish bin by his desk, leaned back in his chair and tried, vainly, for a relaxed pose. 'What makes you say that?'

The uncomfortable look increased. 'I have no concrete evidence. But I do have intuition, Blake, and she was fainting and she looked at me, looked at my tummy and I just know it, Blake. I know it.'

Judith did not get things wrong. He knew to trust her judgment. If she thought there was good reason to suspect anything, then he'd suspect it.

'Early on, I'd say. She's not showing or anything. In fact, I think she's still getting used to it herself. Certainly keeping it to herself—she hasn't told her staff.'

Blake stared into middle distance. Judith's voice faded as he thought about the possibilities. The implications. Then he remembered what she'd said—that she was never having children, that nothing was more important to her than her business. He'd assumed she meant she was covered contraception-wise. A career girl through and through. Just like Paola.

She'd better not be just like Paola.

He swore—short, sharp and loud. He was not going to be shut out again. He was not going to be robbed of all power. He'd get in there and make damn sure his baby was all right. Nothing would happen to another child of his. He wouldn't let it—not this time.

She'd been so adamant about her business being her priority. His eyes narrowed, as did his concentration. This was the business about whose future she was unsure—how unsure? Exactly how honest had she been with him? What the hell kind of game was she playing?

He rapidly reassessed his plan. If what Judith thought was true then Cally Sinclair had no idea what was about to hit her. OK, so this wasn't going to be some nice little beneficial-for-all merger. This was a takeover. And he was quite happy for it to be hostile, because one thing was for sure: he was going to be in control.

'Blake?' He heard his PA's soft voice and when he looked at her he realised it wasn't the first time she'd tried to get his attention.

'Is there anything I can do?' She looked worried.

'No.' He summoned a slight grin. 'Thanks. Head home and rest up. I'll handle things here.'

'It's a few hours off home time, but I'll leave you in peace and find something to do.' She gave him a look but said nothing further, reminding him why he'd given her that rise. Then she stood and made for the door.

'Judith?' She turned to look at him. 'I don't need to remind you about discretion, do I?'

CHAPTER EIGHT

CALLY slothed on the sofa in her favourite raggedy robe and kept pressing the button on the remote. Finally she stopped on a cooking channel, only to press it again when she saw they were doing awful things with offal. She was in such a state of shock she couldn't focus on her computer, or a book, she'd be best off with a lame comedy, complete with cues telling her when to laugh. Ten minutes later she couldn't have told anyone a thing about the show screening. She was kidding herself she was calming down when inside her head there were at least five hamsters competing on treadmills with bells and whistles attached.

The hammering on the door startled her. She heaved herself up, head spinning, made her way to the door and peeked through the peephole.

Damn.

'Open up. I know you're in there, Cally.'

Hell, her insides were going mush-tastic. Her silly heart let out a squeal. Her lower belly began to soften like liquid honey. But her head hit the panic button. She'd fob him off for now. Deal with him when she was on better form. She pasted a smile on and opened the door. 'Blake, what a surprise.'

He too wore a smile but its edges were sharper than a porcupine spike. 'You didn't get my message?'

'What message was that?'

He held up a couple of grocery bags. 'That I'd be doing dinner tonight.'

'Umm…' Stunned, she tried to think. Message? What message? When message? How message? He was here to do *dinner*? Half thrilled, half terrified, totally hungry and utterly too late, she went to decline, polite platitudes finally finding their way to her brain.

He'd already pushed past and was disappearing down the hall. She had nothing else to do but shut the door and follow him. He'd gone straight to her kitchen and was unpacking the contents of the bags onto the island bench. Unsure of what to say she looked at the label on the bottle of wine, brows lifting when she saw the vintage. She glanced up and found him studying her sardonically.

'Why so surprised? I'm not cheap, Calypso, as well you know.'

Her ears pricked. 'Since when do you call me Calypso? How do you know my name is Calypso?'

He took the bottle and lazily started uncorking it. 'Shall we let it breathe a while?'

She said nothing, just kept her stare up, eyebrows still sky high.

The cork came out with a small, satisfying pop. 'I had you investigated.'

'You *what*?'

'Not by a private eye. I wanted to find out more about you. So I got my PA to dig round.'

'Around what—me or my business?'

'Your company initially, but, as you are your company, a bit came up about you too—nothing terribly exciting save the odd rumour… And as you haven't been around to ask I got her to—' He broke off. 'Where've you been these last few weeks, Cally? Not at work?'

'I haven't been well.'

'Oh?' He skimmed over her robe. 'Nothing serious, I hope?'

She ignored the obvious question. 'What rumour? About the company? Food isn't your business. Money is.'

'Your food makes money. You've got a solid performer there.'

'Don't try to flatter me. What's your interest?'

He turned his attention to the bag again, lifted out various-sized containers.

'Calypso.' He mused. 'Calypso—the concealer. Did you know your name meant that? Got anything you're concealing, Cally?'

'It's the name my airhead mother gave me because she wanted something different. I think I'm lucky really. It could have been a lot worse.'

'Hmm. Seems appropriate to me.'

What did he mean by that? She didn't get the chance to ask because he was talking again and she was so surprised to see him all she could do was stare.

'So, have a glass of wine with me. I've got some other delicacies.'

She watched with horror as he poured two glasses full of the deep red wine and then pulled the lid off a tub of marinated mussels. Shellfish. She shouldn't have shellfish. Then he lifted out a creamy camembert so ripe the smell had her gagging.

Quickly she went to the sink and ran a glass of water. Knowing she had to take small sips. Just small or she'd lose it all.

He'd fallen silent, not drinking, not laying out the nibbles, not eating, just watching her with intense focus.

'I'm not really feeling like wine tonight,' she started babbling. 'Not that hungry, actually. Would you mind if we postponed this? I'm afraid I didn't get your message.'

'I thought it would be a nice surprise.' He placed the glasses across from each other on the centre island. 'Don't you like surprises?' He ripped the lid off another container. 'I don't much like them either. And I don't want to postpone this. In fact…'

he stopped moving altogether and simply stared at her—hard '…I think we need to have that chat we didn't have a few weeks ago.'

She just needed to keep breathing, she thought desperately as she heard the steel behind his words. Whatever it was he wanted to talk about, he wasn't going away. Defensive, guilty, she tried to rouse anger that he'd had someone pry into her life. 'I can't believe you had me investigated.'

His body tensed. 'Nothing that isn't readily available. Company records, newspaper articles, financial accounts. You come from interesting stock, Cally. It wasn't hard to find out about you. But, honestly, it wasn't that helpful. I already know things about you that not many others could possibly know. I don't need an investigator to know you intimately.' His voice lowered and his eyes were like lasers. 'I already know how you want it, what you like me to do, how you sound when I do it.'

The reaction in her body was immediate and she ran her fingers across her forehead, obscuring her face so he wouldn't see it. The heat fevered her mind and the temptation to slip her robe off her shoulders was almost irresistible. But it wasn't Blake-The-Playful standing here now and nor was she in any position to resume some frivolous, meaningless sex-a-thon. Clamping down on the desire, she looked back to him, waiting to hear what it was he had to say.

He gestured to the delicacies now spread between them on the bench. 'You sure you won't have some of the cheese? It's really very good.'

If it was even remotely a risk Cally wasn't having it. But he moved to stand opposite her. 'I know you like gourmet, Cally. Have some with me.'

'No.'

'An oyster, then?' He skewered one and waved it in her direction.

'No.'

Something settled in Blake's face. He put the fork down,

placed his hands on the bench and leaned across it towards her. She stood still and tried to ignore how damned attractive he was, fighting the magnetism dragging her towards him and the sweet craving for intimacy.

Looking her square in the eye, he spoke softly so she listened hard. 'I'm nothing if not honest with you, Cally. Can you say the same to me?'

She was hypnotised by his eyes, burning inside, and her newly discovered but most treasured secret tumbled out.

'I'm pregnant,' she whispered and her heart thundered. He was the first person she'd told. She supposed it was right that it be him. She had been going to tell him anyway—some time.

'Congratulations.' He said it coolly but then picked up his glass of wine and emptied it in one gulp. 'How far along are you?'

'Only a little. I only just found out.'

'Only a little? You're either pregnant or you're not, Cally.'

'I am. I'm pregnant.' Even as she said it—to a guy who was looking less than thrilled about the idea—she couldn't stop the thrill running inside. Unutterable delight. She'd never expected to be able to say that, had refused to dream it could or would ever happen. But it had.

He refilled his glass. Took another sip—this time not quite draining the glass but, still, it was no way to drink a bottle of wine that expensive. 'I thought you said you were never having children.' He was looking frostier by the second. She'd known this would probably be his reaction but disappointment jolted her all the same.

'I shouldn't have. The chances of my conceiving a baby are—'

'What, one in six?'

He definitely was not pleased. She knew then to kiss goodbye any fantasy of baby makes three and happy ever after. Blake didn't need to worry; she wanted nothing from him. Well, that wasn't strictly true. She'd thought these last three weeks had got her over that attraction. But one second of seeing him through that door and the all-encompassing desire was back.

But there was a lot more at stake now and she was better off ridding him from her life. She'd swallow the lust and focus on her future—hers and her baby's.

He strolled, with an unmistakable air of menace, around the island separating them, coming to tower over her.

'So what exactly were you bidding for at that auction, Cally? Sperm donor?'

She gaped. 'No.'

'You must take me for such a fool. But know what? You picked on the wrong himbo.' His eyes lasered into her—green-grey chips that burned with their coldness.

He thought she'd done this deliberately?

'You're wrong.' Hell, he was the most astute man she'd ever encountered, but he wasn't getting the truth of this at all. 'When I said I was never having children I meant because I can't. I'm not fertile. At least, I didn't think I was.'

The specialist had said her chances of conceiving naturally were basically nil. She'd have to have treatment first. And she'd never thought she'd bother with that—what was the point? She'd never let someone get that close, not after the humiliation and hurt from Luc. Love and babies and happy-ever-after wasn't going to happen for Cally. She was alone—she had been since she was twelve and she'd thought she would be for ever. But now, incredibly and against all odds, she had a child—to love and to protect.

'You expect me to believe that?'

She blinked. She'd never told anyone about her fertility issues. Not even her mother—she'd gone to the doctor in her late teens with bad period pain and Alicia had thought it had all been fixed with drugs. Not so. In her early twenties she'd had it investigated. Surgery was an option but by then Cally had been crushed by Luc and had remembered too much of her father's pain. So she'd decided to put her job and her charity work and her business ahead of any dreams of a family. She knew how much the fantasy of 'family' could hurt. It was the raw wound she kept well protected most of the time. Cool anger began to bubble under the surface.

'I thought I'd have to have surgery before I could get pregnant.'

He didn't seem to be listening, too busy looking mad. If he'd just give her a second, she'd be able to reassure him he was free of all obligation.

Blake tried to marshal his thoughts. Focus. One thing at a time. 'Tell me this. Is it mine?' After Paola's threats and deceit, he had to be certain.

There was a silence. He met her gaze. Hot, hard, angry. Her mouth opened. And then he saw her hesitate, could see the workings of her brain as she deliberated, contemplating the lie.

His eyes narrowed. *You dare.* The flare of his anger must have been apparent because he saw the second she discarded the idea— the second she looked closely back at him. She gave a jerky nod.

'I had to be sure.'

Her colour was high and she took a deep breath. But he didn't think the likelihood of her calming down any time soon was high.

'You're to see a specialist.' God, he needed to get in control of this situation.

'I already am under a specialist. Do you honestly think I wouldn't be? I never thought I'd get pregnant.'

'Right.' He didn't care how sarcastic and disbelieving he sounded. Of course she'd be under a specialist—she had a ton of money and she'd gone to some pretty interesting lengths to get pregnant. Why hadn't she just had herself artificially inseminated? But, no, she'd wanted to pick the stud herself, from a line-up of the best in town. Blake hated to be used, and right now he felt utterly used.

'You don't need to worry, Blake. This isn't your concern.'

'The hell it isn't.'

'You know I'll do anything and everything I can to ensure this baby has the best possible care.'

'Anything and everything, huh?' He clammed his jaw together and inhaled deeply through his nose, trying to stay on top of a barrage of emotions that was tearing through him. He was the one who'd do anything to ensure the safety of his child—he'd failed once. Now he had a second chance. 'We'll get married as soon as it can be arranged.'

'What?'

'Married.'

The look of shock on her face made him even madder. Did she really think she could get away with this?

'I'm not marrying you.'

'You should have thought about that before you used me to get pregnant.'

'I did not use you.'

'Sure you didn't.'

'I never thought I could *get* pregnant.' She hurried to the table in the open-plan living area, looking panicky—as she should. 'Look, I went to my lawyer this morning. Talked about options. He drew this up for me. If you sign it there'll be no obligations on you. I have money, you know I'm not going to chase you for that. I do want to put your name on the birth certificate, but that's it. You don't have to have anything to do with us.'

Her voice faltered as she looked up from the document and saw the look on his face. If it reflected even half the thoughts he was having she was right to look nervous. He was feeling as close to murderous as he'd ever got in his life. He held out his hand for the papers.

It was a moment before she handed them over, sudden reluctance slowing her down as, wide-eyed, she stared at him.

He looked at the pages of type, flicked through a few while his brain processed and the rage part grew inside.

'Did you honestly think I'd sign this?' He tore it straight down the middle and threw it. The pages frustratingly fluttered soundlessly to the floor so he pounded his fists on the table. He swore viciously at her expression. She *had* thought he'd sign it.

'What kind of an idiot do you take me for? How can you expect me to believe you didn't plan this when you have some twenty page document from your lawyer conveniently stripping me of all my rights?'

Her mouth opened. Shut again.

'We are getting married as soon as it can be arranged.'

'I am not marrying you,' she repeated, clearly alarmed but fighting him still—showing her inner strength. But he didn't have room in him for admiration right now.

'Yes, you are.' He didn't know how he was going to swing it, but no way in hell was he being shut out on this. Not again.

She looked stunned and visibly tried to pull herself together with deep breaths that, annoyingly, drew his attention to her full breasts. His already hard-wound body tightened a notch. Damn if he didn't find her utterly desirable. Even now. Even when he knew how devious she really was.

'We don't need to do anything yet.' She was trying to sound calm. Failing. 'It's so early on.'

'We move on this right away.'

'I don't want people knowing about the baby.' Vehemence flashed in her face.

'Too late.' He took malicious pleasure in informing her. 'It's obvious, Cally. How do you think I knew?'

She looked aghast. 'You *knew*?' Anger shrilled her voice. 'You were tricking me with all the wine and the cheese and the damn mussels?'

'Yeah. I admit it. It was a test.' He stepped closer and put it plain. 'Do you want this baby, Cally? What kind of mother will you be? Can you put someone else's needs before your own or is your life only about you and what you want and when you want it?'

Her hand lifted, palm open, fast as a snake, and she very, very nearly hit him.

But his hand caught her wrist. Held it hard. Satisfaction ran through him. He'd finally succeeded in stopping her from carrying out one of her ill-conceived urges. He hadn't had much luck up till now—she'd got everything she wanted from him. Well, now she was going to get a little bonus she hadn't planned for.

'What happened to your manners, Cally?' he drawled, masking the molten mess of emotion inside.

'Leave,' she muttered.

'No. You're stuck with me now.' His jaw clamped. 'And I mean well and truly shackled.' He felt her body tense to break point. Right now he wanted to break her. Docile and compliant—that would do.

'You don't trust me, do you?' She changed tack.

'Not a jot. And wasn't I right not to? I've never met anyone so calculating in my life.'

'You won't believe that I didn't plan this?'

'Nope.'

Cally let the tension go out of her body, slackening her arm. He let it go immediately. Maybe she could pacify him. 'I'm sorry, Blake.'

'Sure.' Granite incarnate.

'Look, I'm grateful to you for wanting to be here for me. I am. But I don't want or need anything from you.'

'I'm not here for you, Cally. I'm here for my baby.'

She swallowed feeling stupidly hurt by the bald statement. 'You were the one who said it was all a bit of fun. We weren't talking marriage or babies, remember?'

'We are now.'

She stared at him. Saw the hardness in his eyes. The same hardness that had been there when he'd said it that first night. A definite no-go area. There was definitely history behind him, some reason why he'd never intended to marry. Probably a past hurt. Although she couldn't imagine him letting anyone get close enough to hurt him. He was all about surface fun and frivolity—naughty weekends that led to nothing.

But there wasn't *nothing* now. He was all steel and determination and she had to fight.

'You don't want me, Blake. You don't even want this baby. This is about you wanting control of this situation. You're never out of control, are you?'

'Stop and use your brain for just a moment, Cally,' he answered softly. 'I think you'll find you already know the answer to that question.'

Their eyes met and she saw the dark desire, heard the echo of his hoarse cry as he climaxed inside her, the feel of the flood of his life force in her. She closed her eyes as a ripple of remembered ecstasy flowed from her belly out, making her want to…making her want him to…

Stop.

She didn't want him taking over like this—didn't want him taking advantage of her sexual attraction to him.

'This is my baby,' she whispered.

'It's my baby too. That's my flesh and blood you're carrying.' He wasn't going to give an inch.

'OK.' She'd still try compromise. 'We can work out visitation rights. You can see the baby any time you like.' She could do that. Surely he'd lose interest after a while?

'No child of mine is growing up thinking he wasn't wanted by his father. I am this child's father and I will be there for her or him every step of the way. So get used to me being around, Cally, because I am going to be right beside you every minute of this pregnancy and beyond.'

Cally bit hard on the flesh of her inner cheek as she registered the passion, the deep conviction behind his words. Not good. Was that what had happened to him? He hadn't been wanted by his father? Her heart ached and absurdly the urge to embrace him flashed through her. She knew what it was like not to be wanted.

'You can be an involved dad—'

'I am living under the same roof as this baby!' he overrode her furiously. 'Either you live under it with me or I have custody and I will fight to the death for that—don't think for a second I won't.' Every muscle in his body was hard, every word shot out. 'And trust me on this, Cally. When I fight, I win.'

She stared at the stranger in her room. She'd never glimpsed this side of him in that sex-drenched weekend. Then he'd been all about lust and laughter and unbelievable thrills.

She deepened her analysis—suddenly remembering the way he'd won the bet. This was a man happy to take risks to ensure he got what he wanted.

Calculated. Merciless. Driven.

No wonder his company was so successful. No wonder he had the reputation for being such a shark in the business arena. Single-minded, he was able to do whatever it took to ensure he got the result he required.

He was right. She had picked the wrong guy.

Desperately she searched for another way to appeal to him. 'We don't have to marry to get what we both want.'

'What I want, Cally, is for my child to grow up as part of a family.'

That stopped her. Family? From the man who never talked marriage and babies? Suddenly he was talking family?

Anger resurged in her. She knew all about family. About betrayal and loss and how much it hurt when the security you were supposed to get never eventuated. Her parents had married for this exact reason—because her mother had got pregnant. And that marriage had failed—her mother walking out on them less than two years later and leaving her father in one hell of an ugly mess.

She paced towards him. 'How can you honestly marry me? How can you promise to love me? How can you make that vow if you're always so honest? If you always "deliver on your promises"?' Scathingly she quoted him and then braced for the answer.

It was a while coming. When he did speak, it was quietly, deliberately and woundingly truthful. 'You're carrying my flesh and blood. You are the mother of my child. I will always honour you. I will always respect you.'

Components of love perhaps—but certainly not the whole recipe. He would never love her in that true sense. He didn't quite say it, but he didn't have to. She understood he had no other depth of feeling for her and, while it struck at her own dangerously soft heart, at least now she knew her child would have the benefit of two adoring parents. Emotion threatened to topple her, tears burning the backs of her eyes. 'This baby means that much to you?'

'Yes.' He looked at her quizzically. 'Is that such a surprise, Cally? Or is it only women who are allowed a strong parental urge?'

'No.' She shook her head. She knew damn well some women didn't have any kind of a parental urge at all—her mother for one. But her father? Her father had loved her and cared for her and right this minute she missed him more than ever. She couldn't deny her baby the possibility of a relationship as close as that with its own father. That realisation struck deep into her, and that moment she knew her fate was sealed. 'Of course not.'

But while her father had been capable of great love, he'd been capable of deep hurt too. He'd been broken-hearted by her mother—by her blithe betrayal and her rejection of both him and their child. Cally was more her father's daughter than her mother's—she already knew how much she could hurt; Luc had proven that. Since then she'd tried to keep her heart hidden and protected. Unfortunately a little part had crept out under Blake's playful caresses those few weeks ago. She knew she couldn't handle the kind of humiliation and hurt that would come if she ended up falling for him while he felt nothing for her other than a kind of gratitude. She had to keep some kind of distance. Surely she had to say no to him.

But how could she? He'd win; he'd always win. He'd warned her just now and she knew to believe him. And the difference between her and Blake and the situation of her parents was that *both* she and Blake wanted this baby. Whereas her mother hadn't, her mother had wanted money and a name, not a baby to have to care for.

Blake was making it clear he wanted to care for their child. He was determined to be there for it every step of the way—as her father had been there for her. How could she deny her child that?

Cally hid the internal quiver. She was trapped. So much of her didn't want a false marriage, but she couldn't rob her baby of its right to two loving parents.

She'd got a little more than she'd paid for on their wager, but the result was priceless. She'd sell everything to keep her child—her body, her heart, her soul.

Blake studied his bride-to-be and couldn't decide what he wanted more—to shake her or to kiss her. Fired-up fury ran through his veins and he tried to ice it up. He'd been taken for a ride and he didn't like it. But he was back in the driver's seat and there he'd stay—in charge of the situation. He wouldn't let her take the wheel again. They'd marry—a.s.a.p. and then he'd have her there right under his nose.

The sudden thought of Cally warming his bed night after night stirred his blood more. Then came the image of her lush, curvy body growing to bear the burden of his child—her head bent over a baby as she nursed it. The protective instinct rose all powerful. Masculine aggression flowed through his veins.

He would fight like the devil to keep his child, and its mother, safe from harm. He would fight her if she tried to block him, and he was quite happy to fight dirty.

He looked at the anger and uncertainty in her eyes—the passion that made the brown melt and mix with golden flecks. He saw the new bloom of colour in cheeks that had been so pale when he'd first arrived. He stared at her sulky mouth as it parted with her fast, short breaths and felt the pull in his groin. There was one way he could get her to say yes. One way he could get her to scream it.

But desire fogged his brain as well and he needed to keep focused. He'd be better to keep her out of his bed until she was there willingly—utterly willingly and for as long as he wanted. If he stayed in control now, he'd be able to retain the advantage. And he needed to do that until he had her firmly tethered to him.

When Paola had got pregnant he'd been powerless to do anything about it. He was not powerless now. And he'd keep it that way.

Cally had used him but at least she wanted the child. And now she'd got him in the bargain. A little more than she'd banked on, but he knew they could swing it to their advantage. They actually had a lot in common. Not least a sexual drive that matched nicely. Once they were through these negotiations they could have a lot of fun together. He decided to throw the thought into the fire. Test her reaction.

'We deal together pretty well, Cally. You please me. I'm pretty sure I can please you. We can definitely work this out.'

Her breathing hitched again. 'You think I'm going to sleep with you again?'

'I know I want to sleep with you. I'm pretty sure you do too.' He'd kiss her now just to prove it. Hell, he wanted to kiss her hard.

'Why would I want to have sex with you when you're forcing me into marriage?'

'Don't be so melodramatic, Cally. This isn't a forced marriage or anything like it. What we have is a deal. A partnership.'

'One that doesn't include sex.'

He shrugged, inwardly smiling at the heightened colour in her cheeks. 'You can say when it will be but, let me assure you, it will be.'

She opened her mouth and he knew she was about to make the ultimate protestation. He stopped her by laying his finger across her way-too-kissable lips.

'Necrophilia's not my thing. I believe your body will be very much alive and willing.'

Her teeth snapped on empty air.

He was right about this being a deal. That was how to handle it—as a business proposition—albeit unconventional. He could concede her a partnership—eighty-twenty with him holding the majority stake. They both had good business sense. They could make this work. And be satisfied. Very satisfied.

He looked across at her and could see her mentally hunting for a weapon—something, anything to make him withdraw. She was out of luck because nothing she could say would sway him.

Her eyes turned bitter as defeat approached. 'I can't be with someone who'll be unfaithful.'

Black anger blinded him for a moment. God, she could be a bitch. How little she knew him. Well, he grimaced, she had a lifetime to get to know him and how he meant it when he said he was honest. He very nearly swore at her some more, but his jaw clamped when he spotted the vulnerability in her eyes. She could say what she liked, but her eyes always told him the real story. Right now this was one angry woman who was just that little bit scared—that little bit hurt. That little bit got to him. He wanted her to be in his keeping, but he didn't want her hurt or afraid.

He took a deep breath. 'I have never been with more than one woman at a time. And I never will. When I promise to be faithful to you, rest assured, I will be.'

Something flashed in her eyes and he fancied it was disbelief. Fine. He'd prove it. He had plenty of time to. Anger came surging back as he thought of something so distasteful every muscle in his body clenched. 'And I totally expect the same from you.' He thought he knew why the idea was so abhorrent. 'I will not have my child exposed to infidelity or have you parade a string of unsuitable boyfriends before it.'

Unsuitable boyfriends?

Suddenly Cally was the one who was angry. 'I don't cheat.' She forced the words at him.

'Good. Keep it that way.'

She opened her mouth. Shut it again. And concentrated hard on keeping her grip, only just restraining the urge to hit him—an urge she'd only ever had once in her life before, about five minutes ago.

She watched as he too tried to keep his cool. The silence was thick as frustration and sheer rage were mirrored in each other's eyes. And the worst of it was that the primary source of Cally's anger was that she still wanted him. His closeness, his presence had her yearning for him. It was that 'conquering ferocious man' thing again. The place between her thighs was all softness and wet. She wanted to take his hardness deep inside and squeeze the tension from both of them. He was so appallingly attractive—even now. She wanted to rid herself of her extreme physical need by rubbing against him in an extremely physical way. Her breasts felt heavy, her nipples so hard it was almost painful. She pressed the tops of her thighs together trying to get rid of some of the energy by clamping the muscles, stopping the urge to rock her hips forward.

And he knew. The green in his eyes glowed as relentlessly he stared at her. The tension zinged along the invisible cord pulling them together.

'Very alive. Very willing,' he murmured.

She had to suppress it, this almost insane urge to sleep with him. The drive to make him lose control and surrender to her—

because she knew it wouldn't really be him surrendering, it would be her. And how she wanted it—the weight of him as he shuddered in her arms, filling her completely, driving against her, into her—hot, sweaty, hard sex over and over.

No way, no way, no way. He thought she'd tricked him and now he was railroading her into marrying him. She could not, would not sleep with him. Mind over matter.

'I think it's time you left.' Shaking and low, her voice was almost inaudible.

'And it's time you thought through your options. There's only one, you know. I'll be back, Cally.' He swung back and for a second she thought he was going to kiss her. Either that or commit some act of violence. He did neither. Instead he spoke, rough and commanding. 'Take care.'

CHAPTER NINE

BLAKE was back first thing. Demanding Cally find her birth certificate. Unable to muster a hint of defiance so early in the morning when her stomach had her feeling as if she were on a small dinghy in a wildly pitching sea, she simply turned and started walking. He followed her to the small office area, watched as she took her certificate from the filing cabinet.

He watched with a wry smile. 'I knew you'd have your papers in good order.'

She stared back humourlessly.

His smile disappeared. 'I'll drop this in to the register office today with the other documents. We marry a month tomorrow.'

She put her hands on her hips and tried to stare him out. 'You don't want to stop and think about this at all?'

He looked at her as if she were stupid. 'I've done nothing but.'

Cally spent the next few weeks alternately ignoring the situation, and then examining her options in depth. OK, so she was pregnant—frankly that was amazing. The doctor had told her to rest, to try not to worry or stress. She looked around her office. She certainly didn't need any more stress—her job provided more than enough. She didn't have the reserves for a sustained battle against Blake.

She had to admit the way he wanted this baby touched her.

They wanted the same outcome. They could get through this. A partnership, he'd called it. And maybe that could work. OK, she *had* to make it work and so she was not going to mess it up with lustful thoughts. For her health, and that of the baby, it was easier to say yes to him. No more arguments. But no more sex either. The situation didn't need to get any more complicated.

Panic flashed through her. *Please, let the baby be OK*—it was such a miracle. She was almost afraid to believe it was real. She'd do anything for her baby to be OK.

She blanked out those deeply lodged doubts and refocused on what she should do. Time and time again she faced the fact that she couldn't deny her baby the opportunity of having two parents who loved it and who would make whatever sacrifices necessary to provide it with security and love. She wanted her baby to have the kind of relationship with its father that she'd had with hers. She wanted the closeness, for it to feel the comfort she had. Her father had loved her, protected her and cared for her—and she had been crushed when he'd died. And then her mother had let her down again and again. Intuitively she knew Blake would never let his child down.

She couldn't let her child miss out on building a relationship with him. What if something happened to her—what if she died too soon as her father had? If she didn't give her child the opportunity of knowing and loving its father, she would have failed as its mother—especially when its father wanted to be involved so much. Her baby deserved both of them. She had to try to make it work. And Blake was determined to step up to the plate; there was no denying that. He might not love her, but he would love his child. His child deserved no less, and she couldn't stand in the way.

Their marriage didn't have to be the road-crash that her parents' had been—and if she kept it platonic, then the less risk of ruin there would be. They could live together—a business deal for them that would mean love for their child. Surely she could master the desire she still felt for him—to give all three of them the best chance of living together peacefully. She had to extinguish the fire between them, so that it wouldn't have the opportunity to burn the whole arrangement down. He'd admitted this wasn't a love match and she needed to lose any secret dreams of romance and happy ever after.

Besides, right now, for someone who was supposedly her fiancé, he was amazingly invisible. He hadn't been to see her once since coming to get her papers. Well, she wasn't going to go out of her way to see him. She was still half hoping he'd forget about the whole mess—wasn't she?

He didn't forget. Although he didn't show up, he rang, without fail, twice a day—eleven a.m.—she figured it was morning–tea time, and then at night at eight. He was so regular she figured he had an alarm set. Hell, he'd probably programmed his mobile to dial her automatically.

After a few weeks she was sick of it—the twice-daily phone calls that lasted less than a few minutes. He was only interested in how she was physically and what she'd eaten. If it weren't for the baby there would be no contact and even though this was something she already knew, boy, it rankled. She struggled to keep her reactions to him businesslike.

At precisely eight p.m. her phone rang. She answered immediately and before he could even get the 'hello' in she spoke in brisk, bored tones.

'Yes, I had a good day. No, I wasn't sick. Yes, I had a rest in the afternoon. For dinner I had stir-fried beef with Asian greens and rice, washed down with a glass of orange juice, which will help aid the absorption of iron from the meat and veg. I followed that with some fresh fruit salad with Greek-style yoghurt, therefore covering all major food groups so you can rest assured the baby is getting adequate nutrition. Yes, I'm about to go to bed. I am going to read for a while but I'll be sure not to stay up too late. I'll let you know how I slept and what I had for breakfast when you call at the usual time in the morning. Goodnight.'

She didn't wait for a response, knowing she'd neatly summarised everything he wanted to know. It was all about her health—and the baby's. She slammed the phone back onto the receiver, totally irritated.

Fortunately, she had all the paperwork ever generated by her company to work through and—largely—keep her mind off a) worrying about her baby and b) worrying about where Blake was—and with whom—and how she could work her way through this impossible situation.

She'd decided to get everything up to date, knowing the end was nigh for her involvement in the company. While it had been small it had been OK, but with success had come expansion and now it was too big for her to manage alone—especially with her child coming. And she wanted to hand it over completely rather than work with someone else as boss. With her time then freed, she'd explore some of her other ideas.

So during the long daylight hours she went through box after box, file after file, and made sure everything was just right. She compiled lists of contacts and wrote up a guide about the daily processes so that someone could walk in, read it and pick up where she'd left off. If she was going to walk away from Cally's Cuisine, she needed it to be a clean break.

Eleven o'clock the next morning, on the floor in the midst of a pile of papers, she tensed. But her phone sat silent. She wandered over to her desk and stared at it, waiting for it to light up with an incoming call.

Five past eleven—still silent.

Ten past eleven—nada.

Quarter past…twenty past…twenty-five past…

Had she finally got rid of him with her smart-alec spiel last night? For the next two hours she couldn't focus on her work at all—instead she tried to quell the anxiety that something was wrong. Finally her mobile rang. She glanced at the screen. It was Blake. She expelled the biggest breath, then toughened up. She was busy. She let it ring. Two seconds later it rang again.

And then a third time—four, five, six... At that point she switched it to mute and got back to her organising. She only had a couple of last boxes to go through. She climbed up onto her chair, reaching up to the top shelf of her bookcase. She heard the door behind her opening and figured it was Mel. She was utterly unprepared for the loud shout.

'What the hell are you doing?'

She spun on the chair, overbalanced and fell down onto the floor, only just landing on her feet with a wobble and wild waving of her arms. Then she looked up and in a nanosecond registered the tall, muscled man with the blazing eyes and knew that, so far, she was failing in her attempt to get over the lust.

Irritated, she frowned at his glare and her own fear, heart beating hard against her ribs. 'Tidying up my paperwork.'

'You shouldn't be standing up there, for heaven's sake. What if you'd landed badly just then?'

'I only fell because you gave me such a fright barging in here shouting,' she retorted, a little over-defensive because she knew he was right and she had given herself more than a bit of a fright. She launched straight on the offensive. 'Are we still getting married in a few days or are you over that moment of madness?'

'Not madness, Cally—our getting married is a supremely rational decision.'

'I'm amazed you even recognised me, it's been that long since you saw me.'

'Cally...' he strolled towards her, lips twitching—the first sign of relaxation in his tense stance '...have you been missing me?'

'Certainly not.' Good thing she wasn't a little wooden boy with a pointy nose, it'd be six foot long by now.

'Don't you want to know why you haven't seen me? Why I haven't been round every night taking you to dinner and wooing you with flowers and chocolates and non-alcoholic sparkling grape juice?'

If he could be sarcastic so could she and he would never know that a large part of her wished he'd been doing just that. 'I was hoping you'd seen the error of your ways and were distancing yourself so you could retract your crazy proposition.'

'No such luck, Cally, not for you.' He moved closer. 'I've been in New York. I've got a lot of work on over there at the moment.'

'Oh.' She looked at the ground. 'Why didn't you tell me?'

'Why didn't you ask?'

She hadn't, of course. Replaying all those phone calls now she knew he'd done the asking and she'd given him rude, monosyllabic replies. She hadn't asked him a thing.

'I've come straight from the airport.'

She looked at him properly. Saw the stubble, the hint of tiredness in his eyes. She frowned. 'Eleven a.m. here is what time in New York?'

'Seven p.m. and eight p.m. here is four a.m. there. Impressed with my devotion now?'

She flushed.

He pressed home his advantage. 'Seeing you've been missing me, and seeing you've clearly been doing silly things, I think you should move in tonight.'

'What?'

'We're getting married, remember, Cally. You might as well move in with me now.'

'No.'

'No arguments. I'm tired. And I can't trust you.'

'What do you mean?'

'Climbing up onto swivel chairs with wheels on them? How is that in the best interest of our baby? It's unbelievable.'

'Blake, I'm pregnant, not incompetent.'

'Sure. You look like hell.'

'So do you,' she flung straight back. Not quite true, but he certainly wasn't his usual immaculate self.

'We'll sleep better together.'

'I'm not sleeping with you.' The words were out bullet-speed, despite the twist of fire in her belly. She had to keep some control here—but her heart was skittering, her head spinning and everything inside was going soft. It was just as it had been that night at the auction: one look at him and she was practically panting. Not good, because he was the one calling all the shots and she knew if she slept with him again he'd have everything from her. She couldn't let that happen.

'Still fighting it, Cally? Fine. Not in my bed but under my roof. Tonight. I'll pick you up from here, we'll go to your place and you can pack a bag.'

'I've got my car. I'll come to you.'

'I'll meet you at your place and we'll go together.'

He arrived ten minutes earlier than he'd said he would. She was already ready, but made a show of frowning and stalling and all the while melting on the inside with how gorgeous he looked and steaming up with her own weakness. They took his car. She sat and fiddled with the stereo, selecting music that was loud and made speech impossible. He drove in time to the fast beat and in complete control of the powerful engine.

'Welcome home, Cally,' he mocked as he flung open his front door.

'Aren't you going to carry me over the threshold?' she asked tartly.

His head tilted, danger flicked in his brows. 'I don't think our touching is a very good idea right now, honey. Not unless you're saying you're ready for everything.'

For a long moment they stood staring deep into the other's expression. Cally caught fast by the dark glitter in his eyes and the sensual half-curve of his lip. The lust swirling in her belly was almost enough to sway her towards him before she'd even thought about it.

She clenched everything—teeth, fists, pelvic floor—and forced her brain to keep working. Blake wanted her body—

but not her heart. The trouble for Cally was that she suspected if she gave him the one, the other would follow—and soon. Then what hope would there be of making their marriage an equal partnership? He would always hold the advantage.

So she kept a tight rein on her muscles, turned and walked through ahead of him. From then she took great care not to get too close, ensured there was some furniture or decent amount of space between them. Not because she was afraid of him, but because her silly hormone-filled body wanted to be near him. OK, it wanted to jump him. She didn't look directly into his face again—except for once as he held a long glass of juice out to her. The intensity in his eyes was enough to make her beat a rapid retreat up to the bedroom he'd assigned to her, not sure who it was she was really punishing.

She slipped into bed and hoped sleep would claim her. But it refused to make an appearance. She listened with acute hearing to the sounds of Blake as he moved around the house. She was so attuned to him. The night stretched longer and longer and when she woke early the next day she was even more tired than when she'd slid between the sheets the night before.

Then she heard the gentle splash of water—Blake diving in and swimming, length after length. She'd spent the night with her balcony door open, enjoying the fresh air and being able to see the light of the moon on the sea. But it meant she also had a spectacular view of the pool. His strong body powered through the water—tanned and muscular and lithe. At first she tried to lie in bed, hiding under the covers, while he swam, but the images that played in her head were tormenting. So she got up and filled in some time by standing in the shower. Then, inevitably, she was drawn to stand near her balcony door, screened by the curtain she'd pulled almost to the side, and peek out. He was so extraordinarily beautiful. His body was honed to strong, muscular perfection, his broad chest dusted with wholly masculine hair that she could still feel rasping against her nipples as they'd moved together. His thighs were broad and strong and could easily take his weight and hers. She could still taste him. He'd tasted so good.

The sight of him rising out of the water almost did her in—the rush of desire racing through her. He hadn't been kidding. He didn't bother with shorts. And in the morning light, with the drops of water sparkling on him, he looked like the god of virility. Whatever happened to the idea that cold water caused shrinkage?

She had to have another shower—one with no hot water in the mix.

She took to the pool herself later in the morning, when he'd gone to work, when the sun beat down direct on the water, heating it even more than the gas. She hoped the exercise would help her sleep later—but her body wasn't hankering for that sort of exercise.

Blake McKay was one pregnancy craving she couldn't indulge in.

In the early afternoon she was just about to walk out the door when he walked in.

'Where are you going?'

'Who are you? My gaoler?'

He looked put out. 'It was just a question, Cally. This isn't some prison.'

'You think? I'm going to see the specialist.'

Impossibly he looked even more alert. 'I was going to ask you when you were next seeing him.'

'*I'm* seeing *her* today.'

'Great. *We're* going *together.*'

Cally read the implacability and decided not to argue it—besides, he might learn a few things.

At first he sat silent, happy to listen while the doctor ran through some standard info.

'With your condition there are slightly higher risks but—'

'Condition?' Blake interjected.

The doctor looked surprised and looked to Cally for guidance.

'He doesn't know much about it. You explain it to him.'

She sat back and half listened as the doctor talked to him about endometriosis. About the build-up of tissue, the pain it could cause—had caused—Cally, the possibility of needing surgery.

'I hadn't thought she'd be able to conceive without having that surgery first.' The doctor smiled. 'But, miracles do happen.' She eyed Blake speculatively. 'Cally came alone to confirm the pregnancy, but it's great to have you here too. She's going to need a good support person.'

The doctor's glance rested on the unadorned fingers of her left hand. She looked at Blake and saw that he too had followed the direction of the doctor's gaze.

'I'm here for Cally,' Blake said. 'We're very excited.' And he gave Cally a smile that dazzled. But it was the tenderness in his eyes that shocked her into a startled jump on her seat. The smile sharpened and he reached his hand across and took hers firmly in his.

'Well, I'm sure between the three of us we can take great care of Cally and her baby.' The doctor beamed.

At that Blake asked all kinds of questions about her condition and what it meant for the pregnancy.

'There is a higher chance of miscarriage,' the doctor admitted, 'but it's still a small percentage and there's no reason to believe you'll be in that.' She sent Cally a bracing smile.

It didn't reassure her. Wasn't there reason to believe she'd be in that group? Wasn't she the queen of the minority percentile?

She tried to reclaim her hand but Blake wasn't letting go. Rather he held on more firmly and took to tracing the back of her hand with his other fingers. A stroke she knew was designed to soothe but that in reality was, oh, so tormenting— she wanted him to stroke her like that everywhere. She shook away the desire clouding her mind and then found herself gripping onto his large strength, holding onto the bond as she asked the doctor for guidance.

'What can I do to make it be OK?'

The doctor smiled. 'Just try to relax, Cally. Try not to get too stressed. Ease your load off for now. You'll probably get a burst of energy in the second trimester. But until then just listen and rest when your body tells you to.'

'Let's get something to eat.'

She couldn't quite meet the look in his eyes—the sympathy, the apology and the tiny hint of uncertainty. It was the vindication she should be pleased to get. But it didn't please her. Having him look at her like that, with that tender, protective flare, made him all the more attractive. And she couldn't have him become any more attractive. So she wasn't ready to accept his olive branch yet. Not when she didn't have her own feelings under control.

'Actually I promised Mel I'd go in this afternoon and relieve her for a few hours.'

His jaw clamped and she quickly looked away, not wanting to believe she'd just seen disappointment.

She headed back to work at the shop. She swallowed a couple of mouthfuls of soup for lunch and then looked at the ever-increasing piles of paperwork. The sooner she got the place sorted, the better.

Her door opened and Blake walked in. She stared silently as he walked across the room and round behind her desk to stand right beside her.

'I have something for you.'

He held out the small velvet box.

Stupidly, as soon as she saw it her heart and lungs stopped functioning, meaning her reply was totally breathy. Girly. Pathetic. 'What's that?'

'A new plug for the kitchen sink. What do you think it is?'

His acerbic reply had her drawing a deeper breath and with a reluctant grin she took the box from him, battening down her need-to-cling instinct. She opened the lid, and her heart and lungs stopped again. Not good for brain function. 'Blake, it's far too much.'

He bent down and took charge, taking the ring out of the box and jamming it on her finger. 'Cally.' Holding fast to her hand, he looked her in the face and talked. 'When I do something, I do it to the best of my ability. Give it all, all the time. If I take something on I'll make the best of it. It seems you do the same. In that way we might be a good match. I think we match in other ways as well.'

She pulled her hand back while her body screamed to get closer. She wanted him. But she did not want to fall for him. And when he acted like this it was really hard not to. This mess was bad enough without her heart getting soft.

'I'm sorry I was unsympathetic when you told me about your fertility problems. I'm sorry I didn't believe you.'

She shrugged. 'I can understand why you reacted the way you did. But I didn't set out to use you or to trap you.' She was the one who was trapped.

'I know.'

'So we don't need this now, do we?' She looked at the ring glittering on her finger.

He looked grim. 'I'm afraid we do, Cally. The situation still stands. We marry this week. We're having this baby together.'

She frowned, stared at the ring for a long time.

'Do you like it?' He actually sounded hesitant.

The ring? How could she not? 'Of course I do. It's stunning.'

'I wanted you to choose with me but you were determined to come back to work.'

Her eyes flicked to his in surprise and she read faint condemnation there. How was she to know he'd wanted to go ring shopping? He'd just mentioned lunch. Now he made her feel like an ingrate. Oh, hell, this wasn't a normal engagement—why was he messing with it now? They weren't a normal couple in love and unable to wait to get married. This was a business deal because he wanted to be in on the baby and she couldn't let her baby miss out. But his eyes seemed to promise more. Much more.

She couldn't handle that heat so she dropped her gaze—to his mouth. Suddenly she wanted to kiss him. Wanted to thank him—give him an all-the-way-all-over-body thank-you. Silly girl. She should be handing that oversized rock right back to him and saying this marriage was totally unnecessary. But, looking the way he was, she knew initiating that argument right now would be futile. He looked as if he was right on the edge.

'Cally…'

For her own safety she had to push him back from it. 'I'm due downstairs.'

He rose to his feet. Incredibly she realised he'd actually been on his knees in front of her. He paced round her office, full of energy, angry energy. She sat back in her chair and tried not to admire him in action, tried not to turn into malleable jelly. Suddenly he stopped his lengthy strides and gestured to her desk, at the teetering tower that masqueraded as her in-tray.

'Looks busy.'

'It is,' she admitted cautiously.

'Get rid of it.' The words were clipped. 'You said yourself all the management was getting too much for you. Sell out. Keep a hand in as creative advisor.'

Her mouth fell open. Yes, she might have said that, and, yes, she might even be thinking along the same lines, but she wasn't going to let him dictate absolutely *everything* in her life. 'I love my business. I've put a lot into it.'

'You have a baby to think about now.'

Of course she did, but she wasn't going to just throw this one away. She was going to see it right.

His eyes narrowed and his attack sharpened. 'Gourmet soup

is hardly an original idea, Cally. Yours might be flavour of the month at the moment, but in a few months there'll be another competitor. Wouldn't it be better to be under the wing of a big company with the money to push the distribution, boost the marketing, develop the brand and the product?'

'A company that might be happy to pull the plug as soon as it stops making the minimum margins,' she argued straight back, conveniently ignoring the fact that she'd been organising things precisely so she could walk away from it—and soon.

'And wouldn't your employees still be better off? To be part of an operation in which they could diversify, get experience within a national or even multinational firm?'

'With a dehumanising environment? A company that treats its staff like robots? That would make hundreds redundant in one swoop and not look back?'

'A company that can offer good packages should that happen? What can you offer, Cally? Surely your staff would be better off with more of a backstop behind them than what you can give?'

She frowned, searching for another avenue, not wanting him to win all the damn time. 'I don't want it to lose its artisan flavour. Or the gift of a percentage of its earnings to charity. People rely on that.'

'Don't worry, Cally. I can find the right buyer and arrange it, no problem.'

Anger spurted. He could arrange everything—babies, weddings, the works!

She looked at him again and was even more angered to see a small smile playing on his mouth as he watched her.

'You and I want the same thing. We want this baby and we'll do whatever to keep it safe. I'm right. You can't keep working such long hours. You're looking tired.'

Of course she was, because she spent night after night tossing and turning alone in her bed wishing he were there with her. In her.

'You can't do it all, Cally. Not now. Not on your own.'

She knew he was right, she just didn't want to admit it—not now and not to him. He was calling all the shots and she needed to hang onto something for herself. Just for a little while longer until she had her plans for the future in place. Dignity forced her to fight.

'If and when I decide what I'm going to do with the company, I'll be sure to let you know.'

Only a day later Blake was sitting on the deck, meditating over his whisky, when he heard her walk up behind him. He gripped his glass a little tighter. Calypso Sinclair was going out to break him, and she was damn near to succeeding. But he wasn't going to back down. Now he knew she'd spoken the truth about her fertility issues, the protective bit in him was doubly strong. Marriage was the only answer. It was the only way he could keep some control and be able to help her—and their child. She wasn't Paola, she wasn't going to destroy the baby they'd conceived. And he knew that she hadn't set out to trick him—the pregnancy was as much of a shock to her as it was to him, if not more so. But he could not, and would not, let her go. He didn't want his child to miss out on everything he'd missed out on. He didn't want his child to think he didn't care—having a father who didn't care sucked. And he refused to be a father who wasn't there.

But, he had to confess, it wasn't all about the child. All he really seemed to want to do these days was haul Cally into his arms and have his wicked way. His arms ached, really ached, with emptiness. He wanted to hear her again, wanted to watch her as he sent her over the edge.

She stood with her arms folded, staring out across the water rather than at him.

'I'm selling the company. Everything is organised. I'm walking away completely from now. Mel is going to take over the management while we find a purchaser.'

He tried to colour his words as noncommittal as he could. 'Want me to help with that?'

Her reply was equally *faux* uncaring. 'Think you can?'

'Sure.' Of course he could. But of course he wasn't going to rub his hands together and say she was doing the right thing. He'd play it as cool as she was trying to. 'Leave it to me.'

He relaxed a little more into his seat, took a sip of the whisky. He'd known she'd come round to that—she was halfway there before they'd even met. Now her pregnancy had sped up the process. All he wanted now was for her to come the rest of the way back round to him—all the way to him and with the unrestrained passion of that wild weekend. It was just a matter of waiting. Only problem was he didn't know how much longer his body could handle not being merged with hers. It was all he'd been thinking of for weeks now. Surely once they'd done it some more, he could get it into perspective. Right now it was all way out of perspective. He'd never have thought he could be so distracted by lust. But he wanted her to take the initiative. It would be too easy to sway her with kisses—he knew he could, he knew she wanted him—but he didn't want to give her any more ammo against him. If she was coming back to his bed, it would be with her eyes wide open.

She walked to the edge of the pool, then turned to face him. She might look a little mocking, but she couldn't mask all of her inner thoughts. There was that hint of desperation in her eyes that made him tense up all over again.

'Tradition would have it that we spend our last night apart.'

He wired up even tighter, waiting to see where she was going to go with this.

'Won't you be off having some wild stag-night?'

He couldn't think of anything worse. 'I'm not really that into tradition.'

'Ha.' She scoffed. 'This from the man insisting on marriage.'

* * *

Cally tried to face facts. She was a little in love with him. She'd been a little in love with him for a long time—like from the word go. But he couldn't offer her the kind of love she needed. Her father had been crushed by a wife who didn't love him back and here she was repeating his old mistake. It hurt that yet again she had to settle for less—a husband but not a loving husband, just as she had a mother but not a loving mother. But Cally was determined to be a loving mother. It was because she loved her baby that she had to do as Blake insisted.

Damn him for insisting. What had happened to not talking babies and marriage? What had happened to the easy-come-easy-go philanderer she'd seen at the auction? When did he get so white picket fence?

She told herself that now he'd be the last guy she'd sleep with in a million years. Fact was he *was* the last guy she'd slept with. More than anything she wanted to do it again, yet she was determined not to give in. But her cerebral self-preservation message wasn't getting through to her fevered body. She was nearly shaking with need of him. She ploughed on—one last attempt to get him to change his mind. 'I don't think we need to do the wedding thing.'

Silence.

'You know I didn't plan this. There's no need to tie each other up so drastically.'

More silence.

'I'm giving up the company. I can stay in my flat. You know I'm going to do everything right. You don't need to be breathing down my neck.'

Yet more silence.

'Blake?' Her heart thumped painfully. 'You still don't trust me, do you?'

He twisted in his seat, carefully put his glass on the table. 'I trust that we both want what's best for this baby. But I learnt pretty early on that if you want a job done well, then you do it yourself.'

Anger trammelled through her. 'Damn it, Blake, you can be an involved dad. I won't stop you from having access.'

'You won't stop me?' Exasperation poured off him. 'Damn right you won't stop me. Don't you get it, Cally? I am talking one hundred per cent full-on involved in this child's life. Not some guy he sees every other weekend. I will be there every day, for bath, books, bedtime. To practise ball—' He broke off and took a deep breath. 'The sooner we're married, the sooner you'll get used to it.'

Married. She closed her eyes. She didn't know she could ever get used to being near him and not truly having him. She had no idea how she was going to keep herself whole.

'It's a sham, Blake. It will never work.'

He was out of his chair and beside her before she could blink. 'There's this, Cally.' His hands gripped her waist hard and he hauled her to him. 'This will ensure our marriage is no sham. This will make our marriage work.'

At the press of his body hers convulsed. She couldn't mask the small moan that escaped as she absorbed the tension in him—the tightness of his flexed muscles, the ridge of his erection digging into her belly. She had to open her mouth to get oxygen into lungs that suddenly felt a quarter of their usual size.

Time stood suspended as sexual attraction held them in thrall. His eyes had that dark glitter again and she longed to drown in it. Blood pounded faster, driven by desire.

His lips barely moved as he spoke. 'It's still there, Cally, and it's not going away.'

Another tremor ran through her entire body. Shaking with the effort, she suppressed the urges to rock her hips against his, to rake her fingers down his back.

Slowly he brought his head lower, spoke right into her ear, his breath stirring her hair; another millimetre closer and it would be a kiss. Her eyelids lowered, she only just clung to her control.

'How much longer do you honestly think you can fight it?'

If he kept her close like this it wouldn't be long at all, but still she felt compelled to try. She was fighting hard against something she wanted so badly because she knew that what was between them could never be *all* that she wanted.

Breathing hard, she pushed back from him. For a second he resisted, but then his arms dropped and he let her go.

She felt no relief. 'I'm spending the last night at my apartment and don't even think about trying to stop me.'

'The wedding is at three-thirty,' he replied curtly as he reached back to the table for his whisky. 'Show up, Cally. Or heaven help you if you don't.'

CHAPTER TEN

CALLY lay under the bedclothes and tried to ignore the light piercing through the gap in the curtain. She lasted less than five minutes. She was awake. No denying it. And apparently this was her wedding day.

She reached out a hand and grabbed the phone. Hit speed dial.

'What?'

'Mel, I need your help.'

'Why? What's happened?'

'Close the shop and come to my apartment, will you? It's an emergency.'

'Cally, it's ten past six. I'm not opening the shop for another two hours.'

'Great. Don't open it at all. Come straight here.'

When Mel rapped on her door just over half an hour later Cally greeted her in her oldest sweats and a crumpled tee shirt.

Mel looked worried. 'What's the problem?'

'I'm getting married today.'

'What?'

'I'm pregnant. We're getting married at half past three.'

'You and who?'

'Blake.'

'Blake?' She watched Mel rack her brains. 'The auction guy?'

Cally winced. 'Yes.'

'The incredibly hot-looking, super-wealthy, venture-capital auction guy?'

'Yes.'

'Married?'

'Yes, married, all right? To the guy I bought at auction!'

Mel paused and gave her the once-over. 'Not wearing that, you're not.'

A hysterical bubble of laughter escaped Cally. 'What's wrong with it?'

'Hell, Cally, you don't leave me much time.'

'I'm not going to a bridal shop.'

Mel wasn't listening. 'Thank heavens you phoned me. Thank heavens I am a walking encyclopaedia on all things wedding.'

'I'm not wearing a wedding dress. I am too short and too round.' Cally sighed. 'What's the point? I can't do lace and ruffles and nor can I do any slimline elegant number. I'm best off in some sort of suit.' She hadn't thought about it much. Not at all.

Mel snorted. 'Dress to your body type darling. Now let me think for a second—I've seen it. The perfect frock. But which designer…'

Cally watched, fascinated. Mel seemingly had a photographic memory when it came to wedding-dress design and right now she was mentally flicking through magazine pages.

'Got it,' she declared.

'Got what?'

'The Dress!'

'Great—can they make it from start to finish this morning?'

Mel looked aghast and then almost instantly relieved again. 'Sample. They'll have a sample. We'll just pay through the nose for it. Or you will. Offer to. It'll be fine.'

'Mel, I won't fit a sample—it'll be made for skinny people.'

'It can be adjusted.'

Amazingly Mel was right—about everything. She called the designer as soon as she got the number off directory—yes there was a sample, yes, they could purchase it, yes, it could be adjusted on the spot. And when, a little under an hour later, Cally stood in front of the mirror she saw that Mel had been right about the style too.

'It's not too Jane Austen?' As the seamstress made adjustments Cally frowned at Mel.

'You can never be too Jane Austen.'

The empire line dusky pink dress was pretty and perfect and made the most of her cleavage.

'The colour complements your skin tone.'

The adjustments were minor; they had samples in several sizes—including Cally's.

'That was amazingly easy,' Cally breathed as they walked out of the exclusive boutique. 'And with hours to spare.'

Mel looked at her as if she were loony. 'Are you kidding? We've barely started.' She stashed the box safely in the boot and marched her on, on a mission.

'Are you in love with him?'

'Blake?'

'No. The car-park attendant. Yes Blake. This guy you're suddenly marrying.' Mel gave her a sideways look. 'I knew things were hot between you—that was obvious at the auction. But this is really sudden, isn't it?'

Cally smiled. 'Blake isn't one to sit idle. Once he's made up his mind…'

'And the same can be said for you.'

'I guess. Blake and I are both used to getting what we want.'

'And what's that?'

'Our baby.'

'What's he like?'

'The baby? Mel, we don't even know if it's a "he" yet—it's too early!'

'I don't mean the baby. I mean Blake. What's *he* like?'

'Honest to a fault. Clever. In control. Funny. Strong—'

'And incredibly sexy,'

'That too.'

'Cally. I don't want to burst your bubble or anything. But you hardly know this guy.'

'There's no bubble to burst, Mel.' She grinned and hid the little wince. 'What we have is a partnership.'

'A *what*?'

'A business arrangement. The pregnancy was unplanned and we're going into partnership to deal with it.'

'Cally—'

'It's fine, Mel. It is what it is.'

Mel frowned. 'Hell, you can't be my chief bridesmaid any more.'

'Why not?'

'You'll have to be matron of honour.'

Matron?

'God, Mel, I'm going to be huge for your wedding. I'm so sorry!'

Mel laughed. Turned and hugged her and Cally felt a prickle in her eye. 'I'm not. I'm thrilled for you. It's kinda romantic.'

Three hours later not only did they have the frock, but they had shoes, frilly undies, flowers, accessories and had even had a twenty-minute manicure. This meant they had less than two hours to put the lot together.

In her small apartment Cally showered while Mel threw two packets of soup into the microwave and pressed buttons. Then she sat in her robe and let Mel paint a 'natural' look on with seemingly vast amounts of make-up.

Then she wriggled into the tiny scraps of silk, refusing to think about whether she'd be alone to wriggle out of them again. Failing. She wanted. She didn't want—her hormones had her saying one thing, thinking another and doing something else entirely. She couldn't see straight any more. And the source of all her turmoil was Blake.

She stepped into the dress, letting Mel stitch her in as the seamstress had shown; her final touch was to slide into her hair the diamond-encrusted clip that her father had given her when she turned ten. She was sorry he couldn't be there. He, more than anyone, would have understood.

Squaring her shoulders and the suppressing the fleeting melancholy, she turned to Mel. 'Showtime.'

In the taxi Cally dampened the rising nerves and nausea. Half hoped he wouldn't be there. But of course he'd be there.

She thought about heading for the airport instead. But knew, without doubt, he'd follow her. She'd do this now and worry about the consequences later. It was for the baby. All for the baby.

Right?

He was waiting in the foyer, accompanied by a tall, extremely pregnant woman.

Cally recognised her. 'You haven't had your baby yet.'

Faint colour rose in the other woman's cheeks. 'Another week and I'll have to be induced. I'm sorry if I—'

Blake butted in. 'Judith is my PA. She came to your shop under my instruction.'

Cally gave him a frigid look. 'I'd worked that one out myself.'

She watched Judith send her boss an apologetic look and then slip to the side muttering something about checking the paperwork.

Mel gave Cally's arm an encouraging squeeze and darted after Judith.

Cally stood, trying to keep cool, icily cool. Blake was ignoring the frost in her face and taking his time giving her the once over. Her frost stood no chance in his heat.

He took a step nearer and his voice dropped. 'You look beautiful.'

A line she refused to believe. She turned it back on him— a rightful beneficiary. 'You're the one who looks beautiful.'

And he did. In a made-to-measure suit that enhanced the line of his shoulders, the iron hard strength of his chest and tight abs. She knew how tight and strong he was. As everything in her body softened her temper started to fray. How could it be that here she was forced into a life-altering action and all she wanted to do was jump the man who was making everything so difficult? Why couldn't she control this?

'Thank you for coming.'

'Well, you're good at making me.'

She watched the muscles in his jaw flick and realised he wasn't nearly as relaxed as he was making out.

'Don't push me, Cally. Or I'll make you come some more. Here and now and damn the audience.'

'Really?'

She saw the heat in his eyes explode into flames. Saw the hastily checked move towards her, the hand that rose and fell.

'You know I could.'

That was beside the point. 'I don't want to marry you.'

'I'm not that thrilled about it either, but it's happening, so get over it, Cally.'

Afterwards she could hardly remember the ceremony. All she knew was that it went fast and that all of a sudden the officiator was telling Blake to kiss her.

They hadn't kissed since that weekend. Apart from that one moment on the deck they'd barely touched at all. She lifted her head to look at him and was instantly lost in his burning sea-green eyes. There was such depth to them. Anger most definitely. Aggression. Arrogance.

Suddenly there was nothing else in the world but them, no one else in the world but them. The enormity of their actions hit her in a wall of panic. Just as she was about to run, he bent his head and pressed his lips to hers. Immediately she stilled.

It was to be a chaste kiss. Perfunctory. For the camera she'd seen in Judith's hand. But then his hand moved, his fingers sliding into her hair, and she opened her mouth at the exact moment he did and any suggestion it was chaste was ridiculous. His tongue swept into her mouth, staking his claim, asserting the authority. As she collapsed forward, his other arm clamped around her and pulled her hard against his rigid body. Her arms slid up his back, giving in, wanting him, and she felt his fingers twisting in her hair.

It was only when Judith wolf-whistled that they broke apart. Remembered there were people in the room. He kept one hand on her and she realised how wobbly on her feet she was. Concern flashed in his eyes and she shook her head at him. It was the lust making her dizzy. Nothing else.

Cally looked around and tried to cover the crazy way her heart was beating. She wanted to hide the need racing through her veins. One touch had been it. There was no way she wouldn't be throwing herself at him—as soon as possible.

Judith was smiling and still taking photos. Mel was wide-eyed.

Blake slid his hand down her arm and gripped her fingers. Her skin sizzled and all she could think about was the night ahead. He'd take care of her well and good. God, she wanted him to.

Pent-up passion crackled in the air around them.

'Bye, Mel.' She gave her friend a quick hug.

'Are you sure you know what you're doing?' Mel whispered in her ear. 'That kiss didn't look like some business deal to me, Cally.'

'This marriage is about the baby and nothing but,' she whispered back.

Mel gave her such a 'yeah, right' expression and opened her mouth to argue, but Blake interrupted, smiling at Mel.

'I'm taking Cally home now. She looks tired.'

'Oh, yeah, she needs to get to bed right away,' Mel agreed dryly.

Blake's grin sharpened. 'I couldn't agree more.'

* * *

The smile disappeared the minute they were away from the register office, away from the witnesses. They belted into his car and he drove them straight to his place, his hands gripping the steering wheel. Silence all the way. He wasn't as *laissez-faire* about the situation as she'd thought. He looked as irresistibly complex as he had that night at the auction—half joking on the surface but completely tense underneath. Not just a pretty face—there was way more in the depths of him and too late she recognised she knew too little. Her own tension kept her rigid as she tried to deny the soft ache between her legs, the moisture that had been seeping there ever since she'd first seen him in that suit. Damn if she wasn't sick of fighting this attraction. This need. She couldn't and wouldn't deny it any more. It was her wedding night and shouldn't she go for one she could remember the rest of her days?

She'd been holding back in the hope it would keep her head clear and her heart safe. Obviously that had failed. So why not have the cake and eat it too?

He opened the door for her and then slammed it behind him. She turned at the sound. His brows were drawn over fiery eyes.

'Have you eaten?' he questioned roughly.

'I had some soup earlier.' The last thing she felt like was food. What she felt like was him. 'What about you?'

He walked towards her, his energy visible. Her eyes widened and he didn't stop till he towered above her, millimetres away. 'I'm really hungry.'

She blinked slowly. 'You want something with texture and bite?'

His head jerked, a nod. 'Something I can really get hold of.'

Feet apart, she rose onto her tiptoes so her lips almost met his. 'Then what the *hell* are you waiting for?'

His hand clamped onto the back of her head and his other came around her bottom. With ease he picked her up, took a

few paces and pinned her between his body and the wall. All
the while his lips were pressed to hers—hard.

'Feeling angry?' she challenged him the second he lifted his
head.

'Yep.'

She could feel him shaking and suddenly realised he was
on a knife-edge. That he was about to lose it. And she wanted
to make him. 'I am too.'

Quite deliberately she took his lower lip between her teeth
and nipped on it.

He growled and took her mouth in a kiss that was anything
but gentle. Teeth, tongue and lips met and fought as they
claimed as much from each other as they could. Roughly they
kissed and his body pressed harder against hers. She struggled
to breathe but she pulled him even closer. She wanted it all.

She moaned and he groaned. Her hands sought skin, as did
his. He furiously fumbled with her dress.

'Rip it,' she urged. 'I'm not going to wear it again anyway.'

'No,' he muttered. 'It's beautiful.'

'Rip it.'

The surprise in his eyes gave way to dark desire. The tearing
sound thrilled her and after he'd pushed the dress down and
away to the floor she spread her legs more for him. He
paused—for just a moment—and examined the pretty pale
lace and silk underwear. A half-smile appeared. 'Thank you.'

She didn't want to be thanked. She wanted to be taken.
Right now. She grabbed his face in her hands and pulled him
back to her, kissing him with all the frustration and anger of
past weeks and days. In less than a second he was kissing her
back as hard as she kissed him. He ground the length of his
body against hers and she pushed back as hard as she could.
Even with her high heels she wasn't tall enough for them to
meet at the right place. She grumbled her annoyance, arching
her hips to him, straining on her tiptoes to get to what she
wanted. He bent his knees, hands cupping her bottom, and

hoisted her up so his erection could press right where she needed it to be. He muttered as he smothered her throat with kisses. She could feel the need pouring from him as his mouth, teeth and tongue raked her skin. This was what she wanted. Suddenly she felt in control—for the first time in days she had him where she wanted him, shaking before her, passion-crazed. All powerful and all hers.

He wasn't out of his suit yet but she didn't care. She just wanted him there. All the way there. She found herself repeating one explicit phrase. Two words. Short ones. Telling him exactly what she wanted him to do. Demanding him, commanding him to give her what she'd wanted again for these last weeks until now she was at the point where she could think of nothing else.

She breathed it in his ear, over and over until she felt the control in him snap. Until he moved with speed and force— abandoning the attempt to get them naked, just wrenching aside the material that needed to be moved and thrusting hard.

She went to call out, but whatever she'd been going to say was forgotten before the sound emerged. Her arms tight about his neck, she clung on as the ecstasy hit her.

'Like this?' She hardly recognised the harsh voice as his.

'More,' she sobbed. 'I want more.' Oh, she wanted everything. Still riding the crest, her body shuddered around his. Spasms rocked her again and again.

'Good.' He gave it. And there was no more room for talking.

It was the hormones making it more intense. That was it, the reason why she was crazy hot, crazy emotional, almost in tears, gasping in air. Her legs wound round his waist as he pumped into her, filling her so completely that she thought she'd explode from such exquisite sensation. The pressure built again until the pleasure burst through, taking him with her.

She sagged against the wall, legs useless, body humming. He leaned against her, breathing choppy. They said nothing. She just tried to recover.

He stood back for a moment. Kicked off his trousers and boxers, shrugged out of his shirt so at last, too late, he was naked. He stepped forward again, reached for her. Not too late. His body was already hardening again. Clearly he recovered a little quicker than she did.

Still lax, pliant, she let him support her so he could kiss her throat. He eased her down the wall to the floor and then followed, to lie beside her, tracing the thin blue veins visible through the translucent skin of her heavy, swollen breasts.

'Beautiful.' He kissed them and then lower.

She couldn't stop the wriggle of her hips towards his temptingly close mouth. The relief at having had him again flooded her, together with the desire to have him more. Now.

They hadn't even made it from the entrance to his house.

Her energy returned full force. He held back from kissing her intimately and his teasing made her mad again. She pushed and he rolled; quickly she knelt astride him. Letting her hips roll and rotate over him in the sinuous dance they'd been longing to lead for so long. But he wouldn't let her slide onto him; instead his hand moved between her legs, fingers teasing, tickling.

'So hot, Cally.'

'More,' she murmured, and bent to kiss him.

She tasted his smile as he agreed. 'Much more.' His fingers worked and as she moaned he spoke roughly. 'There are no limits on us now, Cally. The night is young.'

The night was never going to be long enough, for she was hungry again. So hungry.

Her knees rubbed against the carpet as she pushed down on him. His fingers dug into the round flesh of her hips, and he held her firm while he pumped up into her, strong deep movements that took her closer to ecstasy.

With eyes that could barely focus she looked down at his body spread beneath her, at the determination and desire in his face. The control he fought to maintain as he pushed her to her limit.

And she couldn't stop the moans, the throaty sighs that came with each breath, each thrust as she absorbed him and abandoned herself to pleasure. Until at last her body crumpled and her mind was blanketed, descending into the dreamless deep sleep of the replete.

'Are you OK?'

With him as her pillow, she looked up at the window high above the front door. His hand swept across her belly. She turned her head to catch his expression. He looked possessive, proud. Cally panicked. Felt guilt and remorse rush through her. She hadn't given the baby a thought in the last hour. She'd been too consumed with lust. Too needy for the strength and satisfaction he could give. She had just wanted, and demanded he give it. All she'd wanted was him. 'I think so.'

And that hadn't been the gentlest sex. That had been wild and sweaty and, oh, how she'd adored every wild thrust of it. Hell, she wanted more even now. And she knew the baby should be fine. The doctor had said sex wouldn't be a risk.

'Still hungry?'

'Starving.' What was the point in lying? She'd tried denial and that only made it worse.

He scooped her up in his arms and they finally made it to his big, comfortable bed.

'I've missed this,' he muttered in her ear as he pulled her close into a sleepy, sensual cuddle.

This. Not her, but the sex—the release. He was a physical man, of course he'd want this. Was that why he'd been so edgy at their wedding? Simple frustration? He hadn't had his usual release? She blocked out the doubting thoughts by using her mouth on him. It was too late for doubt now. Far too late.

The morning after his wedding Blake woke his wife and had more of her. So hot, so tight, sweet and soft. He didn't think he could ever have enough. She'd been so abandoned last night, so wanting. So totally mind-blowing. Cally had come out fighting in a way that had totally rocked him. He didn't want her to disappear under the finishing-school reserve ever again.

'I think, if we're going to make this marriage work, we need to do this on a regular basis.'

She looked at him with eyes that were slightly baleful. 'Don't say it.'

'Say what?'

'That you told me so.'

'What do you mean?'

'Alive,' she mumbled. 'Willing.'

He chuckled. 'I wouldn't dream of it, honey. I'm far too much of a gentleman.'

'You are not,' she retorted. 'But you were right.' She rolled onto her tummy, stretched an arm out to stroke his shoulder. 'We should have done that sooner.'

'It needed to be when you were ready.'

'You could have seduced me.'

'Maybe.' It wasn't as if he hadn't thought about it. He'd come close on the deck when he'd held her close for the first time in ages. 'I didn't want you to resent me any more than you already do.'

Surprise and a frown flashed in her eyes. 'I don't resent you. I know you're trying to do what's best.'

A small tension snapped inside and he smiled at her. It made him realise how much he wanted this to work. How much he wanted his wife and baby to be well and happy.

Family, his family—the idea made him shiver in a part-terrifying, part-tantalising way. He'd never thought he'd get to here. And, OK, it might not be the conventional blinding-love thing, but they had a fair chance of making it work. The fact they were amazing in bed together might just be the thing to tip the balance in their favour.

He hadn't felt this good ever. He'd done the right thing, insisting on the marriage. That last night—when she'd insisted on being apart from him—had been hell. Maybe he should have taken her back to bed sooner, but he'd wanted it to be her move—as it had been that weekend—and he liked the way she'd exploded, ripping into him like that. Taking what she wanted.

Colour now tinged her cheeks and he'd almost believe she was a shy bride. 'I need to get my toothbrush.'

'I'll go.'

Worried she might be feeling sick, he hurried upstairs to her bathroom, looked about for her brush. On the bench next to the toothpaste stood a large glass filled with... He picked it up to inspect more closely. Thinking at first he wasn't right. But he was. A couple of dozen pregnancy tests—the blue lines showing in the little windows.

He turned at the soft footfall. Cally stood in the doorway. The gentle colour in her cheeks had deepened. A lot.

He looked back at the bench and saw another five or so boxes of pregnancy tests. All with two tests in them. Why the hell did she need to do another ten tests? What was going on?

'How many do you need to do? Isn't the morning sickness enough?'

Anger flared in her eyes together with that desperate look she sometimes had but more often hid. 'I told you, Blake. This pregnancy is a miracle. And I can't believe it. I get up every morning and do a test because I can't believe it. And I won't believe it until I'm over thirty-five weeks and this baby is big and healthy and safe and ready to be born.'

She snatched the glass from his hand. Set it back on the bench. 'I don't care if you think I'm neurotic. I cross off every day. Every long, slow damn day.' She sighed, resigned, regretful.

It was as if some greater force had grabbed his spine and was plucking at it malevolently. Suddenly he realised he had no more power than a puppet. 'But you should be enjoying being pregnant.'

'I know.' Her brown eyes reflected longing. 'I wish I could. This is probably it for me. But until I hit viability and well beyond, I just can't relax.'

Instinct made him reach out and tuck her into his arms. Wishing there were something he could do to make things smoother for her. Hating the realisation that there was nothing he could do to ensure everything was going to be OK. There was nothing either of them could do. It was down to fate. Not a nice feeling. Blake didn't like the feeling that things were beyond his control. That might make him vulnerable. That might make him suffer, and Paola had caused him sufferance enough.

'I don't think you're neurotic.' He was the neurotic one with his control thing. He ran his fingers through her shiny hair. 'I think you're brave.'

As he spoke the words the truth of them rang deep. She'd given so much in this last little while. And he saw how much of an iron dictator he'd turned into. He had given her no options. He'd told himself he was going to protect her, but how much help had he been? He hadn't given her the kind of support she needed. Not really. He'd been too busy thinking the worst and fighting off the lust. Now he knew better—that she was honest and that there was no point fighting the lust. It didn't seem to want to go away.

He'd had no idea the degree to which she'd been worrying. God, he wanted to make it all right. He wanted to make everything be all right. But he had no idea how. So he did the one thing that would make them both feel good immediately. He kissed her. Knowing this was one way he could help her. One way he could take her mind off the things neither of them could control and at least give her physical fulfilment.

Later in the morning he sat at the table on the deck, working at his laptop and looking over every so often, like every thirty seconds, to where she read a paperback. She was lazing on a lounger by the pool, wearing a sheer, flowing ensemble that had his blood nearing boiling. He squinted at the computer screen. Focus.

She tossed the book into the water with an overarm throw that really wasn't bad.

He grinned, happy to have the excuse to talk. 'It was that good, huh?'

'It didn't have a happy ending.'

Restlessly she rose and headed towards him. He closed the lid on his laptop with relief.

For the latter part of the afternoon he returned to the office. Figured it was probably a good thing because no way was he accomplishing all he should from home. He wasn't able to take a break from work—not at the moment when he was in the midst of a big deal in the US. But the night with Cally had been more of a honeymoon than he'd dreamed. There was a peace between them now. The deal was done and they were reaping the benefits. And, physically, there were many benefits.

On his return to the house he headed straight to the kitchen from where there sounded bangs, crashes and a hell of a lot of curses.

He stopped in the doorway, blinked at the chaos. Jars, tins, pots, pans, all manner of utensils, in fact he thought it might even be every kitchen utensil he owned scattered from one end of the room to the other.

In the middle of it all stood Cally, clearly hot, sticky and tired. The unmistakable defiance in her face had him pushing pause on the rebuke that had automatically sprung to his tongue.

'I'm working on some new recipes. *Working*,' she underlined. 'And don't you dare tell me I can't.'

He shrugged, refusing to agree to anything just yet. 'Soup?'

'I'm over soup.'

He fiddled with one of the jars of spice. 'What, then?'

'Sauce.'

He shot her a look. 'I like saucy.'

A hint of a smile, but she still looked defensive.

He moved nearer. 'Why are you looking so aggro if this is what you want to do?' He put his arms around her, felt satisfaction when she leaned back to rest against him. 'What's really going on?'

'I need something to do.' She turned in his arms and he pulled her hips close to his. 'I can't just sit around all day wondering if this is the day I'm going to lose this baby. I need to do something to pass the time because I'm so damn scared it's all going to come crashing down around me.'

He read the frustration and fear in her face and instinctively tightened his grip. 'OK, so you're going to potter in the kitchen, then. What's the immediate problem?'

'I need tamarind and some pomegranate molasses and *you* don't have any in your pantry and I don't want to have to drive all the way into the city to get it.'

So it was all his fault for not having a pantry stocked like a three-star Michelin restaurant. His brows lifted. 'Oh, Cally,' he chided. 'Your spoilt-only-child tendencies are showing.'

Her eyes flashed, there was a flush in her checks and most definitely a jutting lower lip. He hid his smile and rubbed his hand up and down her back. 'You're tired.'

She stiffened. 'Don't you dare tell me I can't do this, Blake.'

'Wasn't gonna.' He let the grin out then. 'Ever heard of internet shopping? You know—click the button and they'll deliver?' He walked away from her, reaching round to grab one of the stools from the breakfast bar and lifting it over to the working side of the bench.

'What are you doing?'

'Use the stool. You can sit at the bench and peel and chop or whatever you do, and your back won't get sore and your legs won't get tired.'

'Oh.' She smiled then and looked a little embarrassed that she hadn't thought of it herself.

He pushed aside some of the mess and hoisted her up onto the bench so she was nearer his height, so he could step in close.

'While we're talking projects, I've got another for you.'

Her brows lifted and her smile deepened. Pleasure rippled through him as he saw her relax.

'I've been thinking we should redecorate the small bedroom down from mine. It would make a great nursery. I even have some stuff—wait there.' He strode down to the room, raided the wardrobe and was back in a few minutes, a couple of shopping bags in hand. He started unloading the contents onto the bench, struggling to find space amongst the clutter from Cally's culinary experiments.

She watched him, round-eyed, as nursery playthings and decorations soon took over bowls and boards. 'When did you get all this?'

'When I was in New York.'

He'd gone shopping one spare afternoon. He'd felt an idiot at first but soon got into the swing of things. There was such cool stuff—all the things he'd never had. He grinned as Cally lifted up a solar-system mobile that had a sun that lit up and a remote control to make the planets orbit. She giggled as she read the 'for seven and older' label on the box.

'For our *baby*, Blake?'

'Yeah, but, you know, our child will be *very* advanced,' he teased. 'Besides, we want her to believe she can reach for the stars, right?'

'I'm not letting my son go up in space.'

They both laughed.

He leaned in, feeling closer than he ever had to her. 'You pick the colours and I'll paint the room.'

'Wouldn't you get in painters?'

He chuckled at her amazement. 'I want to do it.' He ran the back of his fingers down her jaw, then lightly down her throat. 'It's that hands-on thing. I like it.'

'You're good at it.'

The way her voice grew husky got to him every time. She might try to hide it, but he always knew when she was slipping under the net that had them both caught fast. But still she tried to pull back.

'I shouldn't be around paint fumes.'

'We can sleep in the pool house while we're working on it.'

We. Warmth—and not just of the lust variety—washed over Cally in gentle, lapping waves. So they'd be sleeping together some more. Working on everything together.

She shouldn't be feeling so absurdly pleased. This was just a phase—the honeymoon period, literally. She shouldn't get her hopes up, her heart endangered. So they did sex well. So they did laughter well—when they weren't arguing. But that didn't equal love—not on his part. She banished the appealing image of him in paint-splattered jeans and tight tee. Honest she did. Instead she focused on him in his current state—the made-to-measure suit, the long-day-at-the-office stubble and the I'm-hungry-for-you-right-now look in his eyes.

CHAPTER ELEVEN

THE ring, ring, ring of the telephone wouldn't stop. Cally lifted her head and frowned at the clock, then reluctantly raised an arm and grabbed the receiver.

'Calypso, darling. I need you and your husband at my house tonight.'

'Mother?' Cally sat up in bed, an uncomfortable sinking feeling in her stomach.

'I heard you got married. Nice of you to invite me.'

'I thought you were overseas. Aren't you?' The discomfort switched into alarm.

'This is the twenty-first century, darling. We have mobiles and airplanes. If you'd wanted me there, I could have been there.' There was a pause and Cally figured her mother was taking a drag on her cigarette. 'I hope you got yourself a decent pre-nup.'

It was the one thing she and Blake had agreed on without argument—only now she hoped she'd never need it. 'Blake has his own fortune; he doesn't need mine.'

Her mother laughed. 'You always were naïve, Cally. Men always need more than their fortune. And his wealth is *nouveau*, isn't it? It's probably the status of your name that attracted him.'

Cally mentally counted to ten. Her oh-so-charming mother was describing herself and her own reasons for marrying

Cally's father—money and social standing, the supposed kudos attached to the Sinclair name. Was it so impossible to believe Blake had married her because he'd fallen for her?

Cally's heart puckered. She knew he hadn't. Her mother hadn't guessed right, but it was true that Blake had only wed her because she had something he wanted—his child.

'Anyway, I'm back now and I'm desperate to meet you and your *catch*.' Her mother's tones fluttered down the phone with false sincerity. 'So I'll see you and your Blake tonight at seven p.m., won't I?'

Oh, hell. Any remnants of ease from the night with Blake disappeared in a pouf. All her doubts magnified. Despite the reality of their relationship, Alicia liked the world to think they were close she wanted to be thought of as 'best friends' with her daughter. In fact, she'd resented the loss of income that had come with her divorce, resented that Cally had inherited everything, and had been irate to learn it had been tied up in trusts until Cally was of age. Cally was sure that was the reason why she'd demanded custody of her when her father had died. Money was the only language Alicia understood, plain and simple. She was the kind of woman who viewed every other woman as a competitor—even her own daughter. She'd been as unsupportive as it was possible to be, with deriding, cruel, undercutting comments all accompanied by tinkling laughter that held no genuine amusement or warmth.

That chill had been in the call too. Alicia was not pleased. Cally lay back under the covers and wished she hadn't answered the damn thing. How on earth did her mother know about the wedding? But her mother always had her finger on the pulse.

She knew she should talk to Blake. They'd never done the parental meeting. How crazy they should be married and hadn't even covered half the basics. But it didn't matter. You didn't need to know someone to the nth degree before you could love them.

And that was what she did. She loved him, was in love with him. With his steadfastness, the security he offered her, his support, his sexiness, his kindness and, yes, even the way he bossed her about. When he was with her she felt capable of anything—that together they could do anything.

But now, alone in his big bed, anxiety twisted up her tummy. She'd suspected this might happen—that if she went back to his bed she'd fall for him completely. She frowned—she couldn't really blame the sex. Forcing herself to face the truth, she acknowledged that it would have happened anyway. She was destined to love Blake McKay. He was impossible not to love.

Seizing courage, she reached out for the phone again and dialled the number he'd given her. Talking to him would reassure her, wouldn't it? Surely he *had* to feel it too? Hope burgeoned in her heart—maybe there could be more to their marriage.

He answered right away. 'Is everything all right?' His worry was evident even in the gruff tones. 'You're feeling OK?'

Sure she was—physically. She pressed her lips together. Of course, he'd immediately worry something might be wrong with the baby. She didn't hesitate long. 'I'm fine.'

'Are you sure? You don't sound all right.'

She wasn't. She was the world's biggest idiot. He'd married her for one reason only—it was all about the baby. 'My mother phoned. She knows we're married. She wants to see us tonight.'

'Fine.' There was a pause. 'Are you OK about that?'

'My mother and I aren't close, but she doesn't like to be left out of the loop.'

'Does she know you're pregnant?'

'No and I don't want her to. Not yet.' The last thing she needed was the hellish reaction she'd get to that one.

'OK. I'll see you at home tonight, then we'll go put on a good show.'

With that terse reply he rang off. She held the phone uselessly, stunned he'd already gone.

A good show. Was that all they really were?

She tried to focus on the evening ahead and put her energy into surviving what would undoubtedly be an ordeal. Cally was unconvinced she'd fool her mother no matter how good a 'show' she and Blake put on. Alicia might be shallow but she wasn't stupid—far from it. She was calculating and knew exactly how to hit Cally in her weakest spot. She always had.

In the late afternoon, after her swim, she dressed with care, conservatively in a black scoop-neck top that clung on the right curves and hung over the wrong ones. She teamed it with black wide-leg trousers and dainty heels. She accessorised with a heavy gold chain, grimacing as she did up the clasp. There was little point in trying to meet the level. Alicia would find fault with something. As she descended the stairs and went to the kitchen to wait for Blake she found him there already.

He watched her entrance and she saw the heat in his gaze. Felt the responding warmth in her cheeks. Maybe she looked OK.

'Will I do dressed like this?' He gestured to the suit he wore so impeccably.

She nodded, unable to speak. He could wear a sack and still manage to make it look designer.

Alicia lived in an apartment in the flashiest area of town. Wealthy—conspicuously so with a ridiculous amount of security. Cally's heart sank as she saw paparazzi lying in wait. Of course, Alicia would always welcome any opportunity to get publicity. Even her daughter's 'on the quiet' wedding. Her heart plummeted further when she saw a limo pull up and deposit a couple of socialites whom she knew her mother patronised.

Blake pulled over several metres from the entrance, away from the photographers. 'Not quite the quiet dinner you thought it was going to be, huh?'

'I'm sorry.' Cally shrugged. 'Mother likes to make the most of any occasion.'

'Relax. It'll be a piece of cake.' He unclipped his seatbelt and turned to study her. 'Hmm.'

'What's wrong?' She didn't need the hint of disapproval right now.

'You don't look like a passion-exhausted bride.'

He wrapped his arm around her, rested his hand possessively on her still slightly narrow waist. The thrill from his touch made her catch her breath. He must have sensed her reaction because his fingers moved, teasing slightly. She saw his grin as his face loomed large. He kissed her—thoroughly. So that when he finally lifted his head away she was breathless and wishing they were back at his house. His hand rested on her knee, fingers drawing small circles—delicious movements that made her want him to inch higher and higher up her thigh. But they stayed there, gently teasing, and the smile on his lips teased too.

She strove for some dignity, wanting to cover the depth of her desire. Pushed him away—far too late and ineffectually. 'You've ruined my lipstick.'

His grin widened as his gaze dropped to her lips—lips that wanted the pressure of his again immediately. 'You don't need lipstick. Your mouth invites the most when naked.' The raspy edge to his voice was the only hint that maybe he wasn't as unshaken by that kiss as he appeared.

She felt the tug of sadness—he had no idea of her inner turmoil right now. There was so much they didn't know or understand about each other, not least their deepest needs and desires. She stole a steadying breath and steeled herself to handle their situation. At least they did do the sex bit well.

As they exited the car and walked towards the doors she blinked at the flashes and inwardly cursed Alicia. If she wanted to live her life out on the pages of trashy magazines that was her decision, but she didn't have to drag her daughter along with her.

Inside the building the security guard escorted them to her mother's suite. The music could be heard behind the closed door. No, this wasn't to be some nice quiet dinner. This was one of her mother's infamous soirées. Where she'd gather as many of her C-list celebrity pals as possible and they'd air-kiss and bitch behind backs.

As they walked through the crowd in the foyer Alicia glided across the room like a golden goddess to greet them. She looked stunning in a simple sheath. With shoestring straps, the dress clung to her figure—the kind of body most twenty-year-olds would be lucky to possess, let alone a woman well into her forties. Her blonded hair hung loose and sleek down her back. She was a true representative of that tall, glamorous Antipodean look, where she'd be as comfortable on the beach as in the boardroom. It was only when you got up close that you could see the faint lines and the cutting edge in the blue eyes.

'Darling.' She embraced Cally in one of those hugs that pretended to be close but where no part of the body touched except hands light on backs.

Her gaze skipped over Cally and went straight to Blake, stopping and staring. 'I can see why you've kept him such a secret. I wouldn't want to share him with anyone either.'

Blake's arm tightened around Cally, drawing her nearer to him. 'We weren't expecting such a turnout.'

Alicia's stare became more of a cool glare. 'I wasn't invited to my own daughter's wedding. You decided to have a small, private ceremony but I thought I'd have the reception for you.'

Cally munched down on the inside of her cheek. Yeah, right. There weren't any of *her* friends here. Alicia wouldn't know who they were. It was all vague acquaintances and useful contacts. The whole thing was just an excuse for Alicia to do the glamour-party thing—and get more publicity.

She looked around—at the clever lighting, the DJ in the corner, the beautiful staff serving the beautiful people. 'You've really outdone yourself, Mother.'

'My daughter deserves the best.' Alicia gave Blake another less than subtle look-over.

Cally watched her mother give her new husband the eye before glancing away as the nausea rose. The room was packed with millions of model types—she'd spent years trying to avoid them but they'd invaded her home. In their presence she'd always determinedly fought against feeling inferior, unattractive and short.

It couldn't get much worse than this.

Good things come in small packages. Good things come in small packages.

Mentally she tried to get a grip, but, no, the mantra wasn't working.

Cally had worked long and hard to get over the insecurities and feelings of inadequacy her mother had foisted on her. And for the most part, she succeeded.

But as she looked around the room every scrap of self-esteem she'd built disintegrated piece by piece. So what if she'd built a fabulous business? Why couldn't she have inherited *something* from her mother—another couple of inches, say, even *fractionally* longer limbs?

'Blake McKay. So it really is you.'

Cally turned her attention back to her husband and Alicia stage-whispered in her ear as the owner of the sultry voice put her hands on Blake's shoulders and pressed a kiss to each cheek.

'Turns out Paola is an old friend of Blake's.' Alicia's smile revealed polished white teeth. 'Funny how small the world can be sometimes. We've been working on a shoot together. She's Brazil's biggest supermodel and really is such fun and *so* beautiful.'

Beautiful wasn't the word. If Paola had been a blonde bimbette Cally might have coped. But she wasn't. She was tall and impossibly slim with even more impossible breasts. Her hair was brunette with lights that Cally could never have no matter how much she paid the hairdresser. And she was looking at Blake with an undeniably possessive, predatory, *knowing* look. Cally quickly glanced at Blake and saw the unmistakable flare in his face—it was an expression he'd never worn when looking at her. Energy sizzled between the two and it was obvious to anyone who cared to look.

At that point, in that suspended moment, when all four of them stood frozen like a tableaux, Cally realised the night could get way, way worse.

'Paola.'

His voice gave nothing away but his body language sure did. His comforting hand at Cally's waist had gone and she sensed the rigidity, the tension in his muscles as he stood beside her.

There was another frozen moment.

'This is Cally.' Alicia directed the newcomer's attention towards Cally. 'Blake, I must introduce you to someone...' With a sly look, her mother had Blake by the arm and was shepherding him away. With his customary charm he was allowing her to, but it wasn't to Cally that he directed his parting glance. He looked straight at the supermodel. Their eyes met on a level that Cally wasn't able to reach or to fully understand. But she saw the glint—the flash of warning. Definitely warning. And then he disappeared into the crowd with Alicia's fingers possessively curling around his arm.

If she looked under the soles of her feet Cally might find the remnants of her heart. She watched as Paola watched after Blake, history written all over her.

An old *friend*? Whatever they had been, Cally would never believe it was just friends.

Not knowing what to say, not wanting to be next to this woman a minute longer than necessary, she coughed, about to excuse herself for a rest room stop. Paola turned and fixed her in place with eyes like daggers.

'So *you're* Blake's wife?' the model asked, incredulous in a *faux* polite fashion. 'Well, you're a brunette, I suppose. He's always gone for brunettes.' She sort of smiled. 'I can understand why you didn't want Alicia at your wedding. Most brides wouldn't want to be overshadowed on their wedding day. Certainly not by their own mother.' Her dagger eyes sharpened. 'He once asked *me* to marry him, you know? I refused, of course, but he wasn't the man then that he is now.'

Fighting for breath, Cally couldn't think of a thing to say. But no reply was necessary, for Paola wasn't done with her damage.

'Of course, I wouldn't have a problem inviting Alicia to *my* wedding.'

Cally intercepted the passing waiter, stared at his tray. The woman had to be on drugs. How could she think that saying such things could be OK?

'This is just fruit juice, right?' Wow. Her voice still worked and wasn't wobbling—unlike every muscle in her body. The waiter nodded and she lifted the glass.

'You don't want champagne?' Paola asked as she took a flute of bubbles.

Cally paused, panicked for a second before a good enough answer came to her. 'I'm driving.'

'You could still have *one*—after all, this party is for you.'

This party wasn't for her. This party was a nightmare. 'I really don't feel like drinking tonight.' That excuse probably wasn't good enough; in this world 'not feeling like it' was inconceivable.

Paola's eyes widened, assessing, as she looked over curves that Cally knew were even lusher than normal. Definitely not good enough.

'He's gotten you pregnant.' There was a long, hideous silence and then her beautiful lips twisted into an ugly smile. 'He's good at that.' She spoke low and in a voice harder than the glittering icy chips that were her eyes.

Cally didn't have the chance to ask what she meant because suddenly Blake was back and again he had no look for her—

all his attention was on Paola. Paola met his gaze head on and smiled a small, secretive, *pleased* smile.

Cally wanted to leave. Just wanted to curl in a ball to hide and wish, wish, wish she'd never met him. The undercurrents of tension were almost more than she could bear and there was so much more going on here that she didn't understand. And she knew she didn't want to know.

'So how did the two of you meet?' Was it only Cally who could hear the malice underpinning Paola's seemingly innocent question?

'At a charity fundraiser,' Blake answered briefly.

'Charity?' Positively bitchy now.

'A bachelor auction, wasn't it?' Alicia dropped into the conversation as she rejoined the group—casual, with a smile and with such malevolent amusement Cally wondered what exactly it was she'd done in a past life to deserve such a mother as this one.

'Oh. You *bought* him. How funny.' Paola's accompanying laughter was shrill.

Alicia's was melodious. 'And quite a price too, wasn't it, Cally? How ironic when you were so mad with me over Luc.'

Oh, she just had to bring that up, didn't she? Cally used peripheral vision to check on Blake's reaction. He didn't seem to have heard. He was too busy looking at the Brazilian beauty.

Cally attempted a smile, felt ghastly and figured the screw of her lips showed it. Too bad.

Blake didn't smile. 'She bought me for one weekend. I bought her for the weekend after.'

'I didn't know there was another auction.' Alicia's brows delicately rose.

'There wasn't. We had our own private arrangement.' For the first time in for ever Blake put his arm around Cally, but she felt no closer to him.

'And I wasn't taking no for an answer.' His hand ran possessively down her arm. Could he feel her goose-bumps? 'Once I'd found her, I could never let her go.'

Cally saw her mother's brows lift even higher in utter disbelief, then she registered the stillness in Blake's body.

He wasn't directing his words at either Cally or her mother. There was a hidden meaning for Paola and he was fixed on her reaction. Equally, she was fixed on him but she didn't seem to be listening. She stepped closer to him, cutting out Cally from her gaze and her conversation.

'You should still be in front of the camera, Blake. You're even better looking now than you were then.'

Cally's jaw dropped.

At that movement Paola deigned to look at her, smiling at her surprise. 'Didn't you know he's a former model, Cally? Sportswear catalogues mainly.' Paola was clearly pleased to be able to inform Cally of another fascinating fact about her husband. 'About ten years ago, wouldn't it have been, Blake?' She looked at Cally with a gloat. 'I knew him very well back then.'

'Great,' Cally replied woodenly. 'In that case I'll leave you to catch up for a bit.'

She only just got to the bathroom before the nausea claimed her. And as she wiped at her face all she could hear was Paola and her less than oblique reference to—what? He was good at getting a woman pregnant? And he'd asked her to marry him?

Cally didn't want to know any more. She just didn't want to.

But, oh, God, she did. And she knew the answers were nigh on going to kill her.

She spent some time in front of the mirror trying not to get distressed but to put on a little armour, failing in both.

He was waiting for her when she finally emerged. Not even a hint of friendly in his face—just fed up.

'I've said you have a headache.'

She did.

'We're leaving now.'

Fine.

CHAPTER TWELVE

CALLY put her bag on Blake's kitchen bench and finally asked the lesser of the burning questions. 'Why didn't you tell me you used to model?'

'I didn't think it was relevant. It's just one of the many jobs I did back then. You want to know about my paper round and my stint as a filleter in a fish factory as well? Should I provide you with a detailed CV?'

She absorbed his irritation. He was bothered—more than she'd ever known him to be. It was that woman. She'd hurt him badly and she still had the power to hurt him. Cally's heart tore in two.

'It's not something I'm that proud of, Cally.' Even his attempt at expansion was offhand. 'That whole thing is not my scene.'

She nodded. Stayed silent. It seemed to irritate him more.

'I'm not that shallow, Cally. I didn't think you were either.'

He reached for a glass and poured himself a whisky. 'Who's Luc?'

So he had heard Alicia's dig.

'An ex.'

'What happened? Why were you mad with her?'

Cally didn't reply.

'Did she steal him off you?'

She could understand why he'd jump to that conclusion, Alicia hadn't exactly been subtle in the way she'd sized him up. 'Quite the reverse—she set him up with me. In fact—' Cally tried to say it brazenly, as if it hadn't cut her through so completely '—she paid for him to go out with me.'

'What?' He was right to sound stunned; it had been unbelievable. Cally had longed not to believe it.

'She thought I was too old not to have started dating so she paid him to go out with me.'

There was a silence. Uncomfortably she knew he understood what had happened. How naïve she'd been. How hard she'd fallen for Luc when all the while it had been a slightly embarrassing job for him—but one that he'd done very, very well. She'd been heartbroken and humiliated when she'd found out.

Cally almost laughed. She'd thought *that* had hurt? She really had been naïve—because the memory of that moment was nothing on the reality of this one.

She couldn't care less what those people thought, or that her photo would be splashed in the pages of tomorrow's papers together with the cute joke about marrying her bachelor bid. What mattered, what hurt, was that she'd fallen in love with Blake, and there was no way he'd ever fall for her. Not if the beautiful Paola was his usual fare. Not when there was obviously such a flare still between them.

'How old were you?' He held his whisky but was too busy watching her narrowly to take a sip.

'Eighteen.' She wanted to move this conversation on. 'So I suppose that's why she thinks it's amusing that I bought you.'

'For the record, Cally, you did not buy me.'

Yeah, sure she hadn't. He'd never have cast her a second glance ordinarily. And if he hadn't found out she was pregnant she wouldn't have heard from him again. He set the untouched glass on the bench and moved around it. She didn't particularly want to define the blaze in his eyes. But the anger, the burn of betrayal, was blinding. He walked to her and she screwed up her heart in self-defence.

'I'm sorry they did that to you.'

She didn't want his comfort. She didn't want to be his convenience. She wanted to be his love. But he'd given his love elsewhere. And even though Cally loved him, would do almost anything for him, she couldn't cope with being second-best.

If they were two damaged people seeking solace in each other's arms, then maybe they could work—as an arrangement in which neither got more hurt. But Cally was over Luc. It had taken until now to realise it but she was—because she was so far into Blake. And if she was with him now, the damage to her would be immeasurable.

Talk about frying-pans and fires.

He reached for her, but the heat of him on her skin couldn't stop the way her heart was icing over. She slid out of his arms. He looked surprised.

Cally bit on her lip. Knowing she shouldn't ask but unable not to. 'She said you once asked her to marry you.'

The loss of colour in his cheeks was almost imperceptible. But Cally saw it all the same. Steeled herself for the answer.

'Paola? She managed to slip that in, in the few minutes she had with you?'

'Is it true?' She knew she shouldn't have asked. He looked remote.

He dropped his hands, turned away, his answer clipped. 'I was young and foolish, Cally. Yes. I asked her to marry me. She refused. I didn't think so at the time, but I had a lucky escape.'

So she *was* why he never talked marriage and babies. She was the one who'd put him off. Because he'd loved her and she'd hurt him. Cally looked at the tension in his body. There was much more to the story, but he wasn't about to share.

'I'm sorry, Blake.'

Cally hurt right through. Clearly he still cared about Paola.

He hadn't been able to take his eyes off her all night. He'd been coiled with tension from the moment he saw her there.

Cally sank fast under the pain and the futility of her love. She'd never be able to match up to someone like Paola. So perfect-looking. She and Blake would be a striking pair. Imagine the babies they would make together… What *had* Paola meant by that comment? She knew she'd have to find out, but fear held her back from asking now. She could hardly bear to consider the obvious question—did Blake have a child already?

He watched her with eyes that revealed little. 'Don't feel sorry for me. It's all in the past now.'

That she didn't believe. And she had no idea where they could go from here.

He reached for his whisky, took a sip and then sighed deeply. He bent his head and contemplated the amber liquid for a long moment.

Cally watched. The hurt, so evident in him, exacerbated her own pain.

Finally he lifted his head, looked at her with a curiously bright expression. 'Do you want to know why I asked her to marry me?'

'No.' Cally tightened inside, the thud of her heart upping in tempo and volume. 'I'm not sure I do.'

'Liar.' He stepped towards her. 'Cally, you are anything but a coward.'

'OK.' She snatched in the breath her lungs were starving for. 'Why did you?'

'You know I didn't have much of a family. It was the one thing I always wanted. My secret dream. The big happy family like you saw on TV and that every other kid seemed to have. Even just one brother or sister would have been good. I was lonely. Mum worked all hours and we were poor and then I was working all hours too and there was no time for any of those nice moments, you know?'

She nodded, not wanting him to stop.

'I got this modelling job—it was good money and I needed money. I fell for Paola—she was in the shoot with me. I fell in a twenty-year-old-boy kind of way. She was beautiful on the outside and I thought that beauty went all the way in. She came from this big Brazilian family and it was this fantasy of everything I'd never had.'

'You still love her.'

'Love *her*?' He looked aghast.

'I saw the way you looked at her.'

He frowned. 'I don't know what you thought you saw, Cally, but it wasn't me looking at her with love. I don't think I ever loved her, not really. It was the idea of her. She was so beautiful and successful and she wanted me? You know, Cally?'

She did—infatuation, the heady way she'd felt about Luc. Nothing like real love.

He sighed. 'She got pregnant. I wanted to marry. I wanted to marry into her big family and have a family of my own.'

He was silent a while, looking tortured. Remembering Paola's words, Cally reluctantly prompted him. Fearful of what she was going to hear. 'What happened?'

He closed his eyes. 'She said she couldn't be sure the baby was actually mine. But, even if it was, she was too busy with her career to have a family and she certainly wasn't marrying me.'

'The baby?'

His eyes opened and told her more than his words ever could. 'She didn't have it.'

Pain and pity hit Cally with hurricane force. Finally she understood him, his need to take charge of their situation. The reason why he'd fought to have her neatly tied to his side. He didn't want to go through that again—the anger and the inability to have any control over the loss of his child.

'I'm so sorry, Blake.'

For a long moment he said nothing, then stretched out his

hand to her. 'Let's go to bed, Cally. Let's forget about tonight. Let's start over tomorrow.'

With a heart that was bursting, she was unable to deny him a thing right now. 'OK.'

The next morning she woke to the gentle splash through the open doors. Stepping out onto the balcony, she freely watched what she'd secretly watched before: Blake in the pool doing his lengths. Waking up, working out. Strong, methodical, capable, he took the pool apart piece by piece. Solid and dependable. He'd been there for her, every step of the way. Even if she hadn't appreciated it initially, she saw him helping, and thinking of her and her baby. He listened to her, he supported her, he sought out solutions. And when he held her in his arms and caressed her, the pleasure was wild.

He'd been so hurt. What she would give to spare him more. She wanted to give him everything.

Certainty settled in her. Her feet moved without her really knowing it, taking her to her heart's desire, to her love. What a fool she'd been to think she could deny it, repress it. Barefoot, she stood by the pool. The concrete was already warm from the early morning sun and kept her toes a comfortable temperature. The hem of her silk chemise fluttered in the slight breeze.

He must have seen her because abruptly he stopped swimming. Stood up, in the middle of the pool, the water lapping at waist-height. Droplets ran from his bronzed body. Their eyes met. He waded to the nearest edge, put his hands flat on the concrete and in one smooth effort pushed up and out. He walked towards her and all the while didn't break the eye contact.

She said nothing. He said nothing. Instead their eyes spoke, and she knew nothing was hidden from him right now.

His breath didn't seem to be easing from ceasing the exercise; in fact it seemed to be coming even more jerkily now.

She reached out her hand, cupped his roughened jaw with her fingers.

'Cally.' He muttered her name, hoarse.

There was no early morning nausea, no fatigue, just the inner glow from the gift she was ready to give him. Whether he understood what it was he was receiving she didn't know, but perhaps he did, because his expression was more tender than ever before.

She stepped forward, lifted onto tiptoe and pressed a small kiss to the column of his throat, heard the catch of his breath and stepped even closer. Maybe her love could be enough for both of them.

She wound her arms around him and they kissed. The wet of his body made her silk cling to them, until he pushed the straps off her shoulders and she wriggled to make it fall.

Somehow they were on the ground, not noticing the gentle grazes from the concrete as they traced over each other, warm and naked in the sun.

His big body was always a welcome challenge to hers, a delicious fullness that she delighted in. She arched a little, easing his entry.

'OK?' he breathed.

'More than,' as he more than claimed her.

Even this early the sky was a deep ocean-blue, framing him like a majestic aura. But the brilliant colour was nothing on the vivid green of his eyes as he gazed on her, seeming to feast on her features.

She ran her hand down his back, making muscles tauten beneath her touch, rejoicing in the fact that for him she was a sensual delight—that he wanted her. Slowly they rocked together, exquisite, slow friction that caused both of them to groan. She adored him, cupping his jaw, stroking his skin, pressing kisses to favourite parts of him—to all of him. Loving him with her mouth, her fingers, her legs as they entwined around and embraced him.

And he held her, touching her, teasing her—his mouth on her breast, his hand twisting in her hair, a rub of his fingers just above the point where they met.

Every movement ratcheted up the eroticism, the feeling of the moment. Until neither of them could cope with slow, intense rocking any more and it became powerful and each time as she arched she gripped him that bit tighter, that bit harder, taking him deeper. She wanted him wholly, utterly in her, and as part of her.

Eyes wide and focused only on him, she watched and exulted as the tension and torture of pleasure began to show on his face and could be heard in his breath—and in hers too as the ecstasy of knowing she could do this to him, with him, made the moment of completion come faster. His green eyes glittered as he saw her smile and he stole the advantage, bending his head and kissing her—his tongue searching so deep and taking what she offered, making her thrilled she had offered it because he was giving too.

She shook all around him and felt him shudder into her. Their screams and shouts muffled by mouths and tongues still locked together. For a long moment their bodies were rigidly clamped tight, sealed fast by spasms of profound sensation. Nothing could come between them.

When at last the waves had calmed, her body softened and let his rest on hers. Silence sat and peace reigned. She had never felt so right.

Slowly, carefully, he picked her up and carried her back inside to his bed.

'Blake…' she called to him sleepily. She wanted to tell him, wanted to thank him, wanted to say all the words—those three words—regardless of risk.

'Shh.' He kissed her. A soft, soothing kiss, before pressing feather-light kisses on her eyelids, making her keep them closed. 'Sleep now. We'll talk later.'

She did as he bid, snuggling down to sleep—the most truly restful sleep she'd had in weeks.

He rang late in the day. 'I'm sorry, Cally, I have to go back to the States.'

'Now?'

'Right now. I shouldn't be more than a week.'

'Oh. OK.' Did her devastation come through the line?

'I'll call you.'

'Bye.' She held onto the receiver for a while even though he'd hung up—as if she wanted to keep the link with him even though it had already been broken. Just a few brief words and he was gone. He really was rubbish on the telephone.

She was so disappointed. Just when things seemed to be working—when they were really opening up to each other—he had to go. She was alone again.

This morning she'd made love to him—offered him everything. At the time he'd accepted it, and had given back—had been making love to her too. She was sure he had. It had felt so good. So right. Not 'just sex'—not any more, nothing like it. While every time they'd been together had been wonderful, this morning's experience had been on a whole other level. It had been so complete.

She'd been going to tell him how she felt but now she wondered if he'd known the extent of her feelings already. Guessed and gone along with the ride, but then stopped her from making a painful mistake—not letting her spell it out because he wouldn't be able to reciprocate. Had he been protecting her this morning from that humiliation in his kind, strong way? He liked her, but he didn't love her—not like that. And now he'd gone away for business. Was he giving her some space, giving himself some space from a wife who he feared was about to cling?

CHAPTER THIRTEEN

ON THE fifth day that Blake had been away Cally decided just to stay in bed. She'd burrow under the covers and pretend she wasn't feeling hideous. Pretend she didn't mind that she'd only heard from him a few times, each call as brief as always. She tried to rationalise. She just had to recognise that they didn't have that sort of relationship. It wasn't a 'real' one. Sure, they were sleeping together. But he was only doing so because it was fun, it filled that physical need and she was the one who he happened to be stuck with.

She was with him because she loved him. And now she wanted more of him, more from him. Like everything. And he didn't have everything to give, not to her.

And even what he could give she loved him all the more for—his company, his humour, his belief in her, his unwavering support. She couldn't walk away from that, but nor could she cope with having only that. She was utterly trapped.

Shivering, she told herself this time apart was good. She could try to get her unruly heart back in order, try to gain the strength to either accept the situation, or to end it.

But she had an ache. She curled in a ball in the bed—missing him deep inside, hurt that he hadn't even asked if she'd wanted to go too.

And then she realised the ache was real. An intense ache that quickly became harsh stabbing pain centred in her core. It spread out in a wave across her body. She tried but she couldn't stretch out. Panic swamped her as she felt the flood between her thighs. She knew what was happening. And the pain her body couldn't stand, her head couldn't stand either. Everything went black.

Blake couldn't loosen the knot of excitement or relax the twist of anxiety that were pulling his innards in opposite directions. He'd called in the taxi on the way from the airport but she hadn't answered. It bothered him—it was almost lunchtime.

He could hardly wait to see her again—he had sped through the work as quickly as possible so he could get back sooner than he'd planned. He totally regretted not taking her with him. But he'd had to grab the flight that afternoon—had had to get over there or lose the deal. And at the time he'd thought a little distance might do him some good. He'd been getting so caught up in her—he had the feeling he'd stepped off into the deep end and he wasn't sure if he was about to sink or swim. So he'd figured some cool-down time would be good. Only he wasn't any cooler—he was on fire, desperate to see her again, desperate to take her to bed.

That morning by the pool, she'd sent him into another galaxy and now he knew he wanted more. More from her, more from them—bizarrely he wanted more certainty, more of that damn good feeling that came from being so intensely close to her. He'd missed her. Hell, how he'd missed her. He could hardly wait to hold her again.

He paid the taxi driver, looked up at the house and moved faster. The curtains were still drawn. The twist of anxiety tightened. Something was wrong. He unlocked the door and called out. Silence greeted him. A quick glance showed him the kitchen was tidy, empty. Adrenalin spiked and he strode up the stairs.

'Cally?'

He'd never forget the sight of her in a heap in his bed. Never forget the agony in her eyes and the wrench in his heart as he saw her body suddenly tense with pain.

'Cally?' Who knew if she heard him? He didn't know if sound actually came out. He scooped her up and held her close, trying not to completely freak when he saw the stains on the sheet, when he felt the wet on his hands.

He didn't remember thinking, just moved. 'It's all right, honey. It's going to be all right.'

'It's not all right, Blake.'

He clutched her closer, listening hard to hear her broken mutter.

'It's too late. It's too late.'

Ignoring her, he bundled her into the car and broke every traffic rule getting her to the private hospital in record time. He'd do anything, anything right now, make any promise, spend however long in servitude to make things OK—to make his baby OK.

Twenty minutes later he stood in the sterile hospital bathroom and washed his hands. He'd been shut out of the room while the doctors took care of Cally. His head was spinning and he refused to accept what was happening. *No, no, no* and *no* again.

But deep inside he knew, as Cally had known. It was too late. Their baby was no more.

Rage gripped him. He had tried, damn it. He had really tried this time. He had done nothing wrong. He had tried to do everything right. And still he had lost.

He'd never thought he could feel more pain, could feel more useless than he had when Paola had made her decision. He'd been able to hate Paola, to turn his hurt and bitterness on her. This time there was no one, nowhere, to direct his anger. So he flipped it on himself.

Guilt added to the self-loathing. He hadn't been there for Cally. He hadn't been able to help her. How long had she been there? Lying in pain and misery. His guts twisted. In shock, he could hardly focus the thoughts swirling round in his head, couldn't get rid of the image of her as she'd lain knotted up in his bed. How he wanted to escape this nightmare.

He slowly dried his shaking hands. Knew he was going to have to go to her. To say something. Do something. But he didn't know what. He couldn't bear the thought of looking into her eyes. Of seeing the depth of his pain reflected there. Of seeing it magnified.

He just didn't know if he had the strength to handle it.

It felt like for ever since Cally had seen Blake. When she did, it was as if he were there but not there, as if he were still distanced somehow, as if she were looking at him through smeary Perspex and she couldn't clear it out of the way.

He looked at her, around the room, at the white of the walls. It was the first time she'd ever seen him at a loss. And that seemed worse than anything.

Finally, from the foot of her bed, he spoke. 'Have you got pain relief?'

For the physical pain? Yes. For the rest of the pain? There was nothing.

She spent the night at the hospital and the next day he drove her home to his house. A couple of hours—days—drifted by. Cally didn't know where they went. Later she stood under the shower for hours and hours, staring into nothing. The noise of the streaming water filled her head and blocked out the screaming thoughts, the pain. Blake wandered in and out of her vision. She could see him; her once steadfast rock was now uncertain, unsure of what he should do.

Then one morning she woke up. Really woke up. He was curved behind her, as always, his arm tight around her, pulling her against him. Was he trying to keep her warm? It was impossible. She was so cold on the inside. And coldly she questioned—what the hell was she still doing here?

She came right out of her introspection and was able to see

part of the world. Able to see Blake clearly for the first time in days. His green eyes, muddier than usual, had shadows under them. His magnificent bone structure stood out, even more striking. She realised he'd lost weight. She realised he was hurting too.

She sat at the table on the deck, unable to appreciate the view to the sea. She had to let him go. The last thing she wanted was him sticking by her out of a misguided sense of responsibility and pity. That she couldn't bear.

'We shouldn't have married. I'm sorry you had to go to so much trouble.'

He stared at her. Pale. Mute.

'I sit here and I wonder. Did I bring this on myself with those doubts? Was it a self-fulfilling prophecy because I just couldn't quite believe it? Why was I given this chance only to have it taken away?' She shook her head slightly. 'Maybe it was just that my instinct was right. It wasn't meant to be. It was just a passing fancy.' A mirage, an oasis in her literally barren wasteland.

He sat silent, clearly stuck for something to say. She felt sorry—she'd meant to make it easier, and here she was making it harder by voicing the questions that constantly nagged her, the questions that had no answer.

She focused on him. She had to release him from this so he could find someone who could give him what he so desperately wanted. Deny it he might, but Blake McKay was made for marriage and babies.

'Maybe we could get an annulment? Or just a divorce. Whichever is quickest and easiest. I'll find out from the lawyer tomorrow. It shouldn't take that long, should it? It's only been a few weeks.'

'Is that what you want?' He sounded as if he hadn't spoken in years.

Of course that was what she wanted. Because it would be what he wanted, what would be best for him. 'It's what's right. It was all only for the baby, Blake. I'm so sorry.'

She glanced out across the water. 'All those things you bought for the nursery. We shouldn't have bought them so soon. Such a waste.' She shook her head. 'No. We can donate them somewhere, can't we?'

She sat, utterly frozen inside, as he listened. Not challenging. Not putting up any kind of fight. She'd been right. It was what he wanted. 'There's no need for us to be tethered together any more. You should be free.'

She would never be free.

Blake ran and ran and ran. The soft sand sucked at his feet, wanting to drag him down. He was already down and his body was burning from the fight. He wanted to punch the demon who had taken his baby from him. He cursed the gods who had done this. Who had allowed this to happen. Horror filled him as he relived the moments with Cally on the deck. When he'd understood how much life had bled from her.

And she didn't want him. Now there was no baby, she had no need of him at all. She wanted to end their marriage, to move out.

He'd sat there stunned into silence. He'd never felt so gutted—as if his heart had just been ripped from his body. So much for not being able to feel more pain. It was only now that she was trying to end it that he realised how badly he wanted her to stay. How much he cared. He wanted to hold her, to cradle her close and cry with her. He wanted to work through this together—not alone, not let her be alone.

He'd let her down. He should never have gone away. He'd been off having a little time out from a situation that had been spiralling tornado-like way out of his control. Why hadn't he seen it all sooner? It wasn't all about the baby. It was all about Cally. And then, when she'd needed him, he hadn't been there. Now she didn't want him there at all.

Just as he'd finally recognised how badly he needed her. How much she *made* his life.

She'd looked to him with her dry, desolate eyes and he hadn't been able to help her. He hit empty air with his fists as he forced himself to go harder along the pristine coast. Raw pain hounded him, making him go further, faster. Until sweat ran in thick trails, stinging his eyes. Until his heart hammered so loudly in his ears and every breath hurt as he dragged it in. Until his body was so pushed to the edge he stood by the sea and retched. Until the only thing he could think of, the only thing he heard, chanting over and over in his head was *Cally, Cally, Cally.*

Suddenly, desperately, he had to see her, to put his arms around her and hold on tight—so tight she couldn't escape, couldn't block him out. He had to break through the wall she'd built in these last few days. He had to comfort her somehow. He had to make her see that as a team they had so much—that it wasn't all just for the baby. That they were good together and should stay together. And maybe, in a while, they could try again. He'd try anything if he had Cally by his side. With her he could be strong. He wanted to share—wanted her to share the tears he knew she hadn't shed, the grief that he also felt.

He had to stop her leaving. He had to talk to her. If they didn't talk, the silence, the unspoken trauma, would tear them apart. He didn't want that. He wanted to make it right—as right as it could be. And he finally saw that so long as he was with Cally, *really* with her, it would all be very, very right. Together they could cope.

At last he had a plan. He'd go back to her now—why the hell was he out running anyway? He'd tell her how much he cared and that he didn't want their marriage to end. Why hadn't he done it before? Why had he been so stupid?

There was the very large, very real possibility she'd throw it all back at him. Not be interested. Not want to listen. And she would destroy him in a way Paola had never had the power to. Cally held absolute power over him. She had his heart entirely. He loved her. He desperately, utterly loved her. He'd been such a blind fool thinking it was merely a convenient blend of chemistry and circumstance.

He was more vulnerable now than he'd ever been in his life or would ever be again. But still he had to take the risk. Because if he didn't it wouldn't be a life worth living.

He ran all the miles back even faster, adrenalin and fear driving him. It had broken his heart that they'd lost their baby. It would break him completely if he lost her too. He ran through the house, up the stairs, back down, into the pool house, shouting and shouting and shouting her name until he was hoarse, all the while knowing.

She was gone.

CHAPTER FOURTEEN

FOR a few moments there, a few days ago, Cally had thought she might have it all—a husband, a baby, a career to create anew. And then, just like that, it fell apart. It was funny how in one moment life could be changed irrevocably. The moment Blake had stepped onto that stage had been the first change. Her miscarriage had been the final.

Now, she'd lost her baby, the miracle she'd thought she'd never have in the first place, she'd given up her company, and she was married to a man who she loved, but who would never love her. Like and respect, sure, but not the all-consuming, deeply passionate love she had for him. In fact their paths would never have crossed if she literally hadn't paid for his attention.

She choked back the emotion. Not going to wallow. Not going there. There were millions in the world worse off than her. She had money, she'd never worry about where her next meal came from...

But the futility, the lack of purpose, the utter despair of her existence ate at her as she marched through the day automaton-fashion.

There was no such thing as a happy ending. Not for Cally. No one had it all.

She drew on her reserves. Thin as they were. She had obligations. And she would meet them. She hadn't been to the shelter in weeks—the longest time she'd ever had away from it. She'd go, if only for a few hours, to a place where she could at least pretend she was needed for a while. To forget her own desolation, try to find her perspective, try to find a way that could be her future. To stand where she'd worked alongside her dad all those years ago, peeling potatoes and having a laugh. How she'd have loved to show her own child the life lessons to be learned there.

The other volunteers greeted her with warm smiles and concern in their eyes. She knew she looked a wreck, and explained that she hadn't been well. Some of the regular drop-ins chatted with her, checked if she was OK, and she felt touched that these people, who were finding their own lives enough of a struggle, still had the strength to be able to ask after her. She made her way to her most comfortable place, the kitchen, and asked to be left to get on with the preparations for the evening meal. Sensing her need for space, the others left her in her own corner, knife, board and vegetables in hand.

She didn't know how much later it was when she looked up, but she was stunned by his white face, hollowed eyes and sweat-filmed skin.

'Are you OK? Are you sick?' Her heart started pumping, strong beats of blood and panic. She'd never seen him look so pale, so physically ill.

'I'm OK. Now.'

He was looking at her with a curious expression. She couldn't figure out if he were angry or sad, relieved or reproachful or what.

'I thought you'd gone. I had to phone Mel. I think she thought I'd lost it.' He took in a deep breath that wobbled halfway. 'I nearly had.'

In that one instant her hope, irrepressible, flared. It soared high and she hardly dared breathe. She tried to squish it. Looking back to the board, she picked up the oversized knife again and sliced it through the onion.

Then the tears prickled. The tears that she hadn't shed in all these dark days. One spilt. She lifted her hand, angry. The stench of onions clung to her fingers.

'Cally.' He grabbed her hand, stopping her from wiping away the tear. 'It's OK to cry.'

It wasn't. Because when Cally cried all she wanted was for someone to put their arms around her and comfort her. She hadn't had someone to do that in years and years. And she didn't want him to do it. She wouldn't take comfort from Blake. The last thing she wanted from him was pity. She wanted his love.

She shook off his grip and thumped the knife back down on the board. 'I'm not crying, I'm chopping onions, and if you want to *help* you can grab a knife and a board and get chopping too.'

He didn't reply, just stood still and watched her for a moment as she massacred the onions. She said nothing, just kept up the onion decimation, just kept a hold on the emotion desperate to escape.

Then he sighed, picked up another knife and found a board, positioned it next to hers and took an onion. He lifted the knife with both hands, as if it were an axe, and struck the onion, splitting it into two uneven pieces.

He nodded. 'I can see the attraction.'

And then the bangs on his board got louder and louder and quicker and quicker until finally he tossed the knife down with a clatter.

'It's not working.' He took her by the shoulders, hard, turned her to him. 'Talk to me, Cally.'

'No.'

'Yes.'

'No!' He wouldn't let go and she threw the reasons at him. 'I can't give you what you want. I can't give you what you need.' She drew in a breath of courage and told him the painful truth. 'I can't give you what you'd love the most.'

He stared, looked shocked and then spoke—softly at first. 'But I want you. I need you. *You* are what I love the most.' His voice started to rise. 'Do you hear me, Cally? Do you understand me?' His fingers tightened on her shoulders. 'It's you that I want. Just you.'

She shook her head, not believing him. 'You wanted our baby.' That was what he wanted. He wouldn't have come after her if he hadn't found out she was pregnant. It had just been a weekend fling, nothing more, not for him.

His face softened. 'I did. Of course I did. But I also want you. I want you more than anything.' He stopped talking, took a deep breath and started again—with slow, precise speech. 'After what happened with Paola, I decided alone was what I was meant to be. I couldn't trust people after that. I had to do it all on my own. So I did. I worked, I made money, I played around and swore I'd never be vulnerable again. I decided I'd never have a family and then bought myself a house big enough for two.' One corner of his mouth turned up at the irony. Then, staring deep into her eyes, he became wholly serious again.

'And then you came along. And even though I was such a jerk when you got pregnant and I didn't believe you hadn't meant to, you put your trust in me. You came to live with me, to rely on me, you trusted me enough to deal with your business, to marry me.' He stepped closer, his hands lifting from her shoulders to frame her face. 'Why would you do that?' His gaze intensified. 'If you have that much trust and faith in someone, if you give them everything like that, then—' he snuck in a breath '—you must love them, right? Even just a little bit?'

He couldn't hide the hope in his expression, or the uncertainty. She realised how vulnerable he was feeling this very moment. Realised just what it was he was asking and how much she wanted him to ask it.

'Is that what it is, Cally?' he whispered.

Her eyes burned. 'I might not be able to give you that family, Blake.'

'Our family is already made. It's you and me. We're more than a partnership, or some arrangement. We're a team, we're a family. Yes, I wanted a baby. I wanted *our* baby and I am so, so sorry we lost it. But we can try again. And we'll try and we'll try and we'll get all the help we need. And we'll do it because if we're together, we're stronger and can face anything. And in the end if we can't have a baby ourselves then we'll foster or adopt or sponsor. You and I have so much to offer. And there are thousands of kids out there that we could help.'

The burn in her eyes was unbearable now, and still he talked right into her face, fast, frantically getting it out.

'What matters most to me is you, Cally. You being with me. Where I can support you and you can support me. Because when we join forces we're better than when we're alone. You make me. Believe in us. Believe in me. Don't shut me out. Let me in. Let's do this together.'

His eyes were burning too, bright, right into hers and shining with hope and passion and pleas.

'Tonight when I thought you'd gone…I nearly lost it. I'm sorry it's taken me so long to be able to see it, to admit it. Please give me the chance. Learn to love me.' His frustration was palpable as he looked quickly round him as if something might appear to help him get through to her. 'God, what can I do…? How can I make you love me the way I love you?'

The fire in him thawed the ice packed deep around her heart and with the melt came the unbearable pain. Tears that hadn't fallen for days and days rose so thick, so fast, so hot and blinding, and she could no longer contain them.

With sudden and unstoppable force she covered her face with her hands and wailed. 'Please mean it. Please. I couldn't bear it if you don't mean it!'

Bending in two, she collapsed forward, hurting too much to be able to stand. His arms banded around her and he eased her to the floor with him when her legs gave way. Uncontrollably the anguish escaped and he pressed her head against his broad chest, holding her tight, gently rocking as the sobs racked her body.

'I mean it, darling. I do. I love you.' He muttered that and more while with his arms and body he gave the comfort and courage she ached for. She listened and felt and hurt and cried and held him as he held her. Until at last, for ever and a bit later, the convulsions eased and she was able to speak.

'I wanted our baby.' Her arms had felt so empty.

'So did I.' He put his head level with hers, his heart on the same plane.

She smoothed the last of her tears from her face, looked at the strength in his and then reached out to wipe the wet streaking his cheeks. 'We'll try again.'

'We will.' He turned his head a fraction and kissed the palm of her hand.

She smiled at his certainty. And then one last, stupid, insecurity twisted inside.

'What is it?' He saw; she realised now he saw everything.

She whispered, 'It was all just a silly bet. I paid for you. You won that weekend from me. You never would have come after me if I hadn't got pregnant.'

'Cally,' he whispered back. 'How did I find out you were pregnant?'

'You sent Judith to the shop to spy on me.'

'That's right. Now why did I do that?'

She looked at him, read the answer in the glow of his eyes, the love in his smile and her last stupid insecurity was banished for ever. But she didn't answer his question. She wanted to hear it anyway.

He grinned. 'I sent Judith after you because I needed information. Because I wanted you again but you'd just blown me off and I needed a way back in. You had me right from the start. Right from the moment I saw you sitting in the audience looking so superior and so damn sexy and I just wanted to shake the smug look off and have you sighing beneath me. Simple as that.'

'And I took one look at you and wanted you to do anything and everything to me. *With* me.' She looked at him in wonder. 'And then I found out there was so much more to you.'

'So much more to *us*,' he corrected. He stood, held his hand out to her. 'Come home, Cally.'

She looked up into his beautiful face, saw how much he had to offer and felt how the warmth of his love filled all the cold and lonely corners within her and nodded. 'I love you.'

She put her hand into his. He curled his fingers firmly round hers. She knew he'd never let go. And nor would she.

EPILOGUE

BLAKE walked in hours before Cally expected. She saw his amused glance take in the mess.

'How's the new recipe going?'

'I'm wearing most of it.'

He walked to where she stood, ran his finger down her cheek and grinned. Her beautiful ten-month-old son had decided a blow a raspberry at the exact moment the spoon was at his lips, splattering moosh right back in Cally's face.

'The child is a rogue,' she muttered, utterly unable to mask her loving indulgence as she turned to scoop up the slop from the highchair.

Blake turned her back.

'He's ungrateful, for sure. It tastes pretty good.' He kissed some of the puree off her cheek.

'What does?' she asked saucily. 'The food I made or the plate it's on?'

He kissed her on the mouth then, a sweet kiss that hinted at sin. 'He's napping?'

She grinned, leaned into his warm, hard body. 'Been down about ten minutes.'

'So we can bank on at least another ten, right?'

'Is that all you have before heading back to work?'

'It's our third wedding anniversary. I'm not going back to

work. I wouldn't have gone in at all if that meeting had been rescheduled properly.'

He took the cloth from her and sponged her shirt, a naughty smile appearing as he dampened the material covering her breasts. 'I think our little lord of the house needs a sister to straighten him out.'

'He does.' She struggled to speak as, instead of helping clean her up, Blake started toying with her now tight nipples. 'Although it might be a brother.'

'It might. That'll be wonderful. And then we'll give them both a sister to worry about.' His fingers stopped their sensual circling motion. She could feel the way she'd phrased it sinking in. '*It* might?' He gripped her arms. 'There's an "*it*" already?'

She nodded. 'I'm pregnant.'

The smile flooded his face with light and happiness and his kiss filled her with joy and lust.

She pulled back while she was still able to think. 'It's early days, Blake, early days.'

'I know.' His smile didn't dim at all—in fact it broadened and he swung her into his arms, baby mess and all. 'It'll be OK. We've done it once—we can do it again.'

He was right. They had. And they would. Whatever challenges were thrown their way, they would handle.

Together.

EXCLUSIVELY HIS

Back in his bed—and he's better than ever!

Whether you shared his bed for one night or five
years, certain men are impossible to forget!
He might be your ex, but when you're back in his
bed, the passion is not just hot, it's scorching!

CLAIMED BY THE
ROGUE BILLIONAIRE
by **Trish Wylie**

Available January 2009
Book #2794

*Look for more Exclusively His novels
from Harlequin Presents in 2009!*

HP12794R